FORBIDDEN TOMES

THE EARTH GRID SERIES BOOK 3

S.A. BECK

This is a work of fiction. Names, characters, organizations, places, events, and incidents are either products of the author's imagination or are used fictitiously.

FORBIDDEN TOMES

ISBN: 978-1-987859-80-5

www.sabeckbooks.com

DELLA MARSHAL HAD NEVER BEEN SO grateful to have a summer holiday end.

Although a bookish sort of person who loved school and reveled in the fact that she was now studying archaeology at Oxford University, she had always enjoyed summer vacation because it gave her a chance to work on excavations and, even better, to nest in her apartment and spend days on end reading without talking to anybody.

But this past summer had seen her excavation director turn out to be a member of a murderous cult, and then another group of crazies abducted an illegitimate offspring of the royal family right in front of her, before eventually abducting her too.

Oh, and there turned out to be a hidden world full of ghosts, black magic, and wizards. And human sacrifice. The human sacrifice had been the icing on the cake. Every single cheap cable documentary she had turned up her nose at had turned out to be true. At least she hadn't seen any UFOs. Yet.

Having her sense of reality torn apart while simultaneously being threatened with death had done wonders for her social anxiety disorder.

So yes, getting back to class would be a relief.

She had signed up for several of the best lectures by Oxford's world-famous researchers—Bronze Age European Prehistory, Intermediate Old English, Scandinavian Medieval History, and Advanced Laboratory Techniques.

A full slate that would keep her mind occupied and take her thoughts away from the disturbing truths she had found hiding beneath mundane reality.

If she tried really, really hard, she might just be able to forget those truths, or at least pretend they didn't exist.

So for that first day back in class in Michaelmas term, a crisp October day after the seemingly endless Long Vacation the university gave its students, Della walked through the center of the university campus with its ornate Gothic spires, its hallowed libraries, and its secluded college gardens. She attended a couple of fascinating lectures, studied the announcement boards to find more events to suit her tastes, and reserved a pile of books at the Bodleian Library, deciding that she would read in the oldest wing, the fifteenth-century Duke Humfrey's Library, instead of the more modern sections that dated from "only" the eighteenth century.

She had no real reason to read there except for the heavy oak beams painted at the height of the Renaissance; the quiet, wooden cubbyholes worn smooth by the elbows of generations of scholars; and the little mullioned windows overlooking the Divinity School gardens.

Heaven.

She didn't even make it through her first day before she got the call.

"Della! There's trouble in London."

She groaned. It was Lucas Lancaster—reluctant occultist, platonic friend, expert furniture maker, part-time farmer, and major pain in the ass. Any time he called with that worried note in his voice, it meant trouble. Big trouble. As in "I'm going to destroy your sense of reality while putting you in mortal danger" kind of trouble.

But Della could never say no to him because... well... she couldn't.

"What happened?" she asked, frowning. She should have made this a video call just so he could see her frowning. Not that it would make any difference.

"Richard has had some trouble. He's down in London dealing with Montague's estate, and there's been a break-in."

Della closed her eyes and rubbed her temples. She felt a headache coming on.

Richard Camilo was an older Afro-Caribbean gay man who would make a perfect friend if he weren't even more sunk into the occult world than Lucas. While Lucas apparently had a Talent for magic but no willingness to participate, Richard had both the Talent and the will—and a few decades' worth of experience and contacts. Montague James was a bookdealer in the occult who had been killed in their last adventure. Della still felt stunned by his death. Her advisor and her slimy crew had deserved what they had gotten, but Montague had done nothing worse than delve into the hidden world in search of knowledge.

And he had been killed for it.

Killed saving the rest of them.

"So, what happened?" Della asked, her sense of guilt dredging up enough willpower to get involved in this lunacy once again.

"Richard took some vacation time to clear through Montague's collection. He's staying down at the house in London. Last night someone broke in."

"Did they steal anything?"

"It's not clear, but he wants us to come down."

Della sighed. Now she really did have a headache.

"Why?"

"Because he needs us."

"He should call the police."

"It wasn't that kind of break-in."

Della went cold. She cut off the call, stared at her phone for a moment, and turned it off.

It was happening again. She was about to get pulled into something she didn't understand and may not survive. Just the way Lucas had said that last sentence told her all she needed to know.

She didn't have any afternoon lectures, so she retreated to her flat at the top of a shared house just off Iffley Road, a couple of miles from the university.

Big mistake. Her buzzer rang an hour later.

"Go away," she muttered as she lay on her bed, trying to lose herself in a book.

The buzzer rang again.

This time she answered it.

"Go away," she repeated. Now that he could hear her, perhaps he'd listen.

Nope.

"Let me in," Lucas's voice said through the intercom. "This is important."

Ugh. Would he ever leave her in peace?

She buzzed him in, opening the door and glaring down at the tall man in his late twenties as he ascended the steps. His shoulders took up almost the whole width of the narrow staircase. Rough hands hung slack at his sides, hands covered in calluses from long days on the farm and in the woodshop. That lumbering, assured body held a quick mind. People tended not to see that at first. There was a lot more to Lucas once you got to know him.

Della crossed her arms, feeling irritated. "I was beginning to enjoy some normalcy."

He gave her a sheepish grin. "Did you get to the point where you had convinced yourself that all the spirits and spells were in your head and had rational explanations?"

Della suppressed a shudder. No, she hadn't been able to do that.

"Come in," she said, although she wanted to say the exact opposite. "Would you like a cup of tea?"

He shook his head. "No, we need to go."

Della sat on the sofa, Lucas taking the chair opposite. Della studied him. An Englishman refusing a cup of tea? This really must be serious.

"So tell me what you know," Della said.

Lucas ran his fingers through his blond curls. "Not much. Richard called a couple of hours ago. I tried calling you immediately, but you didn't pick up."

"That's because I was in a lecture. You know, normal life?"

"Someone of your innate magical Talent doesn't get the luxury of a normal life."

"That sounds like your aunt talking."

Lucas smiled. "She loves you to pieces. You'll have to come up to the farm once all of this is over."

Della's eyes narrowed. "Once all of what is over?"

Lucas stood. "Let's go. We can get the Oxford Tube down to London. It's quicker than driving. You know how the traffic is down there. And the parking is hopeless. Pack an overnight bag."

"Hey, wait! I'm not spending the night down in London. I have a lecture tomorrow."

Lucas looked her in the eye. He had pretty eyes. Very blue. Della found them as attractive as she found his personality annoying.

"Richard said he's felt some spirits in the house the past few days. At first he didn't think much of it, since it's such an old house and the spirits didn't emanate any malevolence, but this morning he found the books and manuscripts he had been sorting had been disturbed. One was moved, as if the spirit had tried to take it. An important book on magic."

"A spirit tried to steal one of Montague's books."

Lucas nodded.

It was a tribute to how much her life had changed in the past few months that she didn't laugh in his face.

Instead, she felt like curling up in bed with the lights off and waiting for it to all go away.

Della stared at Lucas. Lucas stared back at Della.

"Damn you," Della muttered.

Lucas shrugged. "Sorry."

He didn't sound sorry.

"So why do you need me?"

He grew more serious. "You know why."

Right. Because I'm supposed to have this big Talent for magic.

Without another word, Della packed her bag.

Once she and Lucas took the bus down to London and then the Underground to the Georgian-era house in Bloomsbury that had once been Montague's, things only got worse.

The burn mark on the living room wall was unmistakably shaped like a person.

It looked like the shadow, somewhat fuzzy at the edges, of a person of middle height. Della guessed it was a man but could not say for certain. The image looked like it was caught in midstride, coming *out* of the wall.

Della, Lucas, and Richard stood staring at it. Richard hadn't said anything when he let them in, only ushered them into the living room and let them see for themselves. The house was now in trust to Richard until he could arrange a sale. Briefly, Della wondered what this new addition would do to the property value.

"You didn't mention *this* in your call," Lucas said.

"I didn't want you to worry," Richard said. "Would either of you care for a cup of tea?"

"I need one," Della said, her voice husky.

"I daresay so do I," Lucas said.

Richard went off to the kitchen, humming a cheerful tune and leaving the other two staring at the wall. There were no burn marks on the carpet in front of the wall nor on the sofa just next to the figure. Richard had informed them that there were no other burn marks anywhere else in the house, except for one little spot he would show them in a minute.

"Would you like Montague's special calming blend?" Richard called from the kitchen.

"Yes," Della and Lucas said in unison.

When he came out with a tray, a teapot, and three cups a few minutes later, Della and Lucas were still staring at the burnt figure.

"You two need to get out more," he said in a singsong voice. "Haven't you ever seen a spirit mark before?"

"How about you stop making foolish small talk and tell us what happened?" Lucas asked.

"My, my, a bit grumpy today, aren't we? Della, you should really give him a back rub every now and then. He needs to relax."

Della was too stunned to take the bait. She sat on a

chair at the corner of the room opposite the figure. It was as far as she could get without actually leaving the room. Leaving the house would be a better idea, she mused, or the city. Lucas found another chair equally far away. Richard chuckled and sat on the sofa, making a point of sitting at the end closest to the figure.

"How are you two going to reach your tea?" Richard asked as he poured.

Della and Lucas stood, retrieved their tea, and moved back to their seats.

"So," Richard said, taking a sip. "Ah yes, quite tasty. I have to analyze this blend to find its secret."

"Um, Richard?" Della asked.

"What? Oh, right! Our spiritual burglar." He raised his teacup in a mock toast to the burn mark. "Well, I've been down here for a week now. I would have come sooner, but there was so much to arrange with the burial and his financial affairs, which were in as much of a mess as his house. As you know, I've been coming down most weekends to clean up the place, and I do say that I've worked *wonders*. It's almost habitable. The books, I must admit, I have been putting off until I could take some time off from work and really dig into them. There are simply *thousands* of them. Not only the ones he had for sale, but his own collection. It's been maddening trying to sort them out."

"Didn't he have them organized?" Lucas asked. "He put out a catalog, after all."

"You remember how Montague was. His mind didn't work the way a normal person's does. He had his own filing system that I have yet to decode. Books on entirely different subjects are shelved together. It doesn't make any sense. I don't know how he could find anything in his own library, and yet every time I visited, he could pluck a book off the shelf without a moment's hesitation."

Della nodded. The man had been a first-class weirdo. A brilliant weirdo, though.

"Could we get to the part where a spirit leaves a burn mark on the wall?" Lucas asked.

"You really do need to learn patience, my dear," Richard scolded. "I was just getting to that. So, I have been here a week, and at night I have experienced some ghost activity."

"Ghost activity?" Della asked. Her knee-jerk reaction was to scoff, but then she glanced at the figure on the wall and said no more.

Richard shrugged. "The usual sort of thing—a sudden cold feeling, the sensation of being watched, footsteps at night once or twice. The footsteps were a more serious affair, and of course, I investigated. We are sitting on a literal gold mine here. The collective value of these books runs into the hundreds of thousands of pounds. When I checked, I found no burglars, and the burglary alarm Montague installed works perfectly. So, no humans have been making those noises, at least no living humans."

"Has Montague tried to get in contact?" Lucas asked.

This time, Della did roll her eyes. He asked as if Montague was away on holiday and had promised to call. Richard replied in an equally casual tone.

"No, he hasn't, and I haven't tried to get in touch either. Montague made so many friends, and enemies, in the spiritual world when he was still with us that I suspect he's quite busy in his first few months on the other side. I didn't want to disturb him. So I think this is a different spirit, or spirits. To be honest, I didn't pay it much mind. So many years of occult activity in this house must have left numerous spiritual traces. It could be one of any number of ghosts or entities."

Lucas gestured at the wall. "This is of a rather higher order."

Richard grew more serious, nodding somberly. "That happened last night."

Della plucked up the courage to cross the room and study the image more thoroughly. The wall was simple wood paneling, painted white. The image appeared to have been seared on with a uniform heat, dropping off in temperature at the edges as if the figure had been radiating heat slightly.

She had seen figures like this before, in fact, an entire collection of them.

It had been on a study trip to Rome in her junior year of undergraduate studies. She was taking some classes on classical archaeology at the American Academy. As usual, she hadn't made any friends, being far too shy. When the others would go off together to eat pizza or drink wine, she would go on solo walks through Rome's historic center, enjoying a quiet, thoughtful time only slightly marred by the realization that her solitude was enforced by her own social anxiety and was not something of her own choosing.

She had visited all the museums and ancient sights first, of course, but that summer was so filled with long walks that she began to branch out to see examples of Renaissance art as well. One day, after visiting the Vatican, she was strolling along in the late afternoon when the crowds and the hot Italian sun had become tiring. She took refuge in the cool interior of a church called the Sacro Cuore del Suffragio next to the Tiber River. Its neo-Gothic facade had fooled her into thinking she'd see some nice old church art, and she was disappointed to discover the church had been consecrated in 1921 and the interior was decorated with paintings and an altar in the modern style. Still, it offered a welcome respite from the packed, sunny streets.

And then she found the Purgatory Museum.

It was in a side room right off the nave, a simple display along one wall of articles of clothing, books, and pieces of furniture with burn marks on them in the shape of hands. Puzzling through the Italian descriptions on the displays, Della had learned that the marks had supposedly been made by souls suffering torment in Purgatory.

These supposed visitations were common in the Catholic world from the seventeenth to the nineteenth centuries and took on a regular pattern. Someone who had recently died would appear to a relative or their local priest and tell of the sufferings of Purgatory, which were equal to those of Hell except for the hope of it eventually ending. The spirit would then beg the person to say prayers or pay for masses to be performed to reduce the amount of time the poor soul had to suffer before being brought up to Heaven. To prove that the spirit had been there, it would touch some object with a burning hand, leaving a mark that would then be shared around in public to rally people to pray for the departed.

Della had not been impressed. It sounded like the script from a bad B movie with special effects to match. Most of the burning hand marks didn't have the proper proportions of hands. Some of the burns were simply of fingertips and looked like someone had put down a cigarette in the wrong place. On closer inspection, Della had noticed that some of the images, such as a hand and a cross mark supposedly left on a table by the late Abbot Olivetano of Mantua in 1731, were made up of a series of circular burn marks as if made with the tip of a fat cigar.

Della now studied the image on the wall in front of her, hoping to find a similar pattern. While she didn't think Richard had faked it himself, there were plenty of crazies in the London occult community who were up to such a thing. She tried to ignore the prickling of her skin as she drew closer to it.

She didn't see any evidence of shapes within the silhouette, no repeated marks from some hot instrument. The black mark was uniform except for some fading at the edges. She pulled out her phone and turned on the flashlight function, turning the harsh beam this way and that so she could look at the mark from all angles.

Della took a sniff. It carried a faint tang of burning, and something else.

It took her a moment to realize what.

Brimstone.

Suppressing a shudder, she backed away.

She turned to find Lucas and Richard studying her.

"Find anything of interest?" Lucas asked.

"I don't know how this was made."

"A fire spirit can manifest in many ways," Richard said. "Some of the more malign ones spark fires when they come onto this material plane. It's a good thing this one didn't. With all these books, this place would have gone up like the Hindenburg."

Della decided to let that one pass. She didn't have anything to say anyway.

"So you didn't hear or smell anything?" Lucas asked.

Richard chuckled. "No, I slept like a baby. When I came down this morning for breakfast, here it was."

Lucas rose and walked over to stand next to Della and study the mark. "And you didn't notice any manifestations the previous evening?"

"None. That was unusual since I've experienced at least some sort of low-level manifestation every night since I got down here."

"Interesting. What about during the day, on the weekends when you visited before?" Lucas asked.

"Never. I hadn't slept over until I came down on vacation this past week. So whoever is moving about here at night, they don't have the strength to materialize during the day."

Della would have really, really liked to have scoffed at this entire conversation. Unfortunately, she was trapped by the overwhelming evidence of previous experience.

"You said this isn't the only trace?" Della forced herself to ask, dreading the answer.

It turned out that she was right to dread the answer.

Richard smiled. "No, there's another little treat the spirit left me. Come this way."

"Why are you smiling?" Della asked as he led them into a back room. "If this had happened to me while I was alone in a haunted house, I'd be terrified."

I'm scared enough as it is, and I'm here in broad daylight.

"I find it invigorating! I've never seen a spirit

mark this pronounced before. Something major is about to happen. I can feel it. You and Lucas can feel it to, although you're both too stubborn to acknowledge it. It's like a crash course in spiritualism. I learn so much more from something like this than from six months of reading."

I'd rather take the six months of reading and leave off the human-shaped burn marks.

Richard brought them into a back room. Della remembered it from her previous visit during the summer, when Montague had still been alive.

She felt a tug of sadness to see the lumpy armchair in the far corner, its old cushions still impressed with the outline of the bookdealer's lanky frame. How many hours, days even, had he sat there reading esoterica?

All around the chair stood piles of books, still where Montague had left them. On a side table were heaped even more. In fact, the whole room was overflowing with books in tidy piles or random heaps. Only a narrow path led through them to the armchair. Della remembered the whole house was like this. Richard would need a lot more than a couple of weeks' vacation to sort through this mess.

The occultist moved to one corner, where a

coffee table was visible only as a shift in terrain amid a landscape of books.

Then Della saw what he had been talking about.

At the center of the table lay a book bearing three burn marks on the cover. Burn marks in the shape of fingers.

2

THE BOOKS on the coffee table were all older volumes, bound in heavy leather or even vellum. Unlike the rest of the room, these piles looked orderly, as if Montague had treated them with special care. All except for the burned book. It lay at an angle, as if someone, or something, had tried to move it.

Lucas Lancaster stood by Della as they examined the book from a safe distance.

"Is there a ward on this book?" Lucas asked. He could feel the prickle of magic nearby but wasn't attuned enough to the invisible world to know exactly what he was sensing.

"There's a ward on this whole table," Richard

replied. "These are some of the most valuable books in his collection."

"Then why aren't they in one of the glass cases in the library or upstairs?" Della asked, skipping the whole interaction about wards. Lucas figured she really didn't want to know. Poor girl. She'd have to learn sooner or later.

"They're recent acquisitions," Richard said, "bought in an estate sale in Scotland. He had them here because he was going to put them in his next catalog, the one he never got to put out."

Lucas felt a heavy weight on his heart. Poor Montague. He had never really liked the bookdealer —he was far too strange and antisocial—but he certainly hadn't deserved his fate.

Glancing at Della, he saw tears well up in her eyes.

She doesn't want this. She doesn't want to be a part of any of this. She just wants her life to go back to normal.

Sorry. Not going to happen in this lifetime.

She was special, far more special than Lucas, with his limited understanding of magic, could say. Some great, hidden Talent for manipulating the unseen world was buried deep inside her. A Talent that had saved their lives more than once.

Not Montague's life.

That's probably what she's thinking about.

Lucas put a hand on her shoulder as tears rolled down her cheeks.

"Are you all right?" Lucas asked.

She shrugged off his attempt at comfort.

"I'll be fine," she said, her broken voice belying her words.

Everyone stood there quiet for a moment until Richard broke the silence.

"The spirit moved through the house until it found this book. When it tried to move it, the ward activated and sent it back to the spiritual plane. I'm not sure if it wanted this particular book or one of the ones under it. Perhaps it wanted several books. All of them are worth thousands, if not tens of thousands. This is the crème de la crème of one of the better occult libraries. The researcher died some months back."

Lucas turned to him. "Not Frederick MacHugh up in Orkney?"

Richard nodded. "The same."

Lucas turned back to the table, eyes going wide. His aunt had talked about MacHugh many times. He was one of the greatest practitioners in Scotland, an old man who had spent his entire adult life studying the hidden world. In his youth, he had known such figures as Aleister Crowley and Gerald Gardner. The man had been taught by the best. Aunt Mary always spoke of him with awe.

The books on this table were very valuable indeed.

Valuable enough for some powerful sorcerer to send a spirit to try and steal them.

And he or she would be sure to try again.

"What's the nature of this ward?" Lucas asked.

"It is specifically against any sort of magic being cast on the books, indeed the entire table. That includes any manipulation from spiritual beings. Montague must have anticipated something like this."

"And not regular people breaking in?" Lucas asked.

"You mean regular occultists," Della said with a snort. "Bookish recluses with pipe cleaner arms?"

Lucas raised an eyebrow. "I beg your pardon?" He was as surprised by her quick improvement of mood as he was in her cutting remark.

Della smiled. "Present company excepted, of course."

"And the cult at the King's Stone."

Della's face darkened. "Them too."

How quickly your mood can change.

"I did have a couple of attempted break-ins," Richard said. "Amateur fumblers who on both occasions tripped the burglar alarm. One tried to come through the garden window, and the other tried to pick the front door lock. Got a good shot of both of them on CCTV and recognized them from London meet-ups. I called the police and brought them up on charges. Both are beginners, in occultism and in burglary. I didn't really want to involve the police, but I thought it might set an example to the rest."

Della nodded. "It did. It made someone send a spirit instead. Seems odd to send a fire spirit to fetch books."

"Some fire spirits only burn at will, or when manifesting, or when getting hit by a ward. But yes, it's still an odd choice. That might have been the only spirit available to them. Could be a clue as to their identity."

Lucas turned back to the books. "Any clues which of these could have been the target?"

Richard shook his head. "No. All of these are rare, all of these are valuable, and in the wrong hands, most of them are highly dangerous. And as for your other question, physical break-ins will probably not be a worry. There's a good burglar alarm and several locks and bolts on each door, and the windows are bulletproof glass. It helps that this is a safe neighborhood with regular police patrols and good CCTV coverage."

"Municipal CCTV doesn't count," Lucas said. "That's more to get fuzzy, unidentifiable images of the suspects once they've made their escape."

"True enough," Richard said and chuckled.

It was a safe neighborhood, however. Montague's house stood just west of the British Museum on Bedford Square, a beautifully preserved Georgian square with housing prices that were considered exclusive even for London's hyperinflated real estate market. While crime was rife in the capital, a formidable amount of wealth ensured that not much happened in this postcode.

"So now what?" Della asked.

"Just what you've been looking forward to, milady," Richard said with a mock bow. "An occult ritual to see what we can discover about our nocturnal visitor. We know little about him except that he's quite a flamer, which makes him near and dear to my heart."

Della rolled her eyes.

"I asked you down," Richard continued, "because you have more natural Talent than anyone I know, and that's saying something. Also, because I need four people for this task and Lucas is a dear, dear friend who is always willing to help in a pinch. More willing than before, at least. Getting him out of his shell is harder than opening an oyster with a plastic knife."

"Wait. You said you needed four people," Lucas said. "Who's the fourth?"

Richard suddenly looked uncomfortable. "Um, well, I needed someone with Talent, someone who knew Montague, and someone who could be trusted in the house with so many rare books lying about."

"And who would that be?" Lucas asked, a rising feeling in his gut telling him he already knew the answer.

Richard took in a deep breath. "Cassandra." The look on Lucas's and Della's faces made him hurry on. "Most London occultists with real Talent can't be trusted! You know how this city has attracted too many practitioners of black and gray magic. And the cost of living! Lots of people in our community are financially struggling, and here we are sitting on a whole clutch of golden eggs. Who else could I have asked?"

Della raised a hand as if asking permission to speak in class. "Anyone in the known universe?"

"Sorry, but no. We need a local with Talent,

knowledge, and experience who can be trusted. And besides the people in this room, that leaves her."

"Is the London occult community really that bad?" Della asked.

"Oh, honey, you have no idea. This city has always been a nexus for the greedy and power hungry, and occultists are no exception. Some are quite mad."

"Worse than Montague?"

"Montague wasn't mad, just highly maladjusted," Richard said.

"I'll say," Della replied. "He was always baiting you with homophobic and racist remarks. Remember when he called you 'the slutty spook of supernaturalism'? You're telling me that was just some form of social awkwardness?"

Richard laughed. "It was indeed. Real racists and homophobes either thump you in the gut or smile in your face and snarl at your back. I'll take silly remarks from an honest social outcast any day. Montague was a saint compared to some of the characters you find in local circles."

Lucas had to agree. Aunt Mary was always pestering him to learn more about the magical arts. Sometimes, when he had to deliver one of his handcrafted pieces of furniture to a wealthy client in

London, he'd stay the evening to attend a talk at one of the city's many local occult meet-ups, usually held in the back room of some dodgy pub or the cellar of an outré bookshop. He'd met a whole range of psychotics, megalomaniacs, white supremacists, and slightly unsettling, unwashed nutters. He'd even met a flat- earther who, sad to say, wasn't the least sane in the bunch. The scene here was a world away from the kind of people Aunt Mary had over for her rituals. They were all pleasant, older suburbanites or village folk you'd expect to find tending cabbage and carrots in an allotment rather than drawing magical circles and summoning spirits.

The doorbell rang. Lucas's heart sank. Glancing at Della out of the corner of his eye, he saw her frown and cross her arms.

Wonderful, Lucas thought. *I'm stuck dealing with my ex while Della goes into a pout. Well, might as well get it over with.*

He followed Richard to the front hall. A small video screen on the wall showed a video from the CCTV installed right above the door. Cassandra stood there, waving at the camera and blowing kisses. Her blond hair shone in the autumn sunlight. Her pert features and perfect skin told of good breeding and a life of privilege.

Why did it have to be her? I'd rather be on the way to my own beheading.

Richard disabled the alarm, pulled back the chain and two bolts, and opened the door.

"Darlings!" Cassandra said, giving Richard a hug and air kisses. She did the same to Lucas, who stood there stiffly, hoping Della wasn't there to see.

She wasn't. In fact, she was nowhere to be found.

"I do hope I'm not late," Cassandra said as she flounced in. "There's been some trouble at the office."

"More cuts to Thames Water?" Richard said.

Despite growing up rich, Cassandra had studied urban engineering and was now one of the city's chief water engineers. She was as intelligent as she was superficial.

Cassandra's face took on an expression of mock surprise, her big blue eyes going round. "Why, of course. It's an essential service. You can't expect the government to resist the temptation to cut funding for the third year in a row."

"I did sense a certain increased mealiness to the tap water," Lucas said.

Cassandra put a hand on his arm. "Darling, I work for Thames Water, and I only drink bottled. That should tell you something."

She left her hand on his arm. In fact, it began to move up.

Della chose that moment to make an appearance.

"Oh. Hello," Della said.

"Della! How grand to see you!" Cassandra exulted, giving her air kisses.

"If I had known you were coming, I would have brought those clothes you lent me after I took a dive in that sewer."

"Oh, don't worry about it."

Della managed a smile. "I gave them a good wash, and I've resisted the temptation to wear them since. The blouse and pants were especially nice."

"Keep them if you like," Cassandra said with a wave of her hand. "I had set them aside for the charity shop, if they would have them."

Good Lord, Lucas thought. *She's not acting like that already.*

Richard saved the day. "Righto. More tea, and then I'll catch Cassandra up on current events."

After an awkward tea, during which Lucas and Della kept silent as Richard repeated his account of the previous night's events, Cassandra took some time studying the marks, passing her hands closely over the surface of both outlines.

"No residual magic," she murmured. "Montague's ward blasted the thing right back into the spiritual plane."

"I felt that too," Richard said. "It's nice to see the old boy knew how to protect his stock."

"So, did he leave them all to you?" Cassandra asked. Lucas could hear a bit of envy in her voice. She had been born to a wealthy family and enjoyed a lucrative career, and because of that, she had always been overly obsessed with the finer things in life. It was one of the many things she and Lucas did not see eye to eye on.

"No, he put it all in trust to me, providing me a stipend so I could get his affairs in order as well as a list of books that he gifted me. Some quite choice ones, tailored to my interests. Very kind of him. The rest, along with the house, I'm supposed to sell and give the proceeds to various charities. Libraries and literacy efforts for the disadvantaged, mostly."

"He wasn't an old man," Lucas said. "I'm surprised he had his affairs in order. I don't even have a will yet."

"That's because you don't have a penny to your name, darling," Cassandra said. "Those chairs and bureaus you make are quite lovely, but they will hardly buy you a Georgian house in Bloomsbury."

Lucas thought of several cutting comebacks and

decided not to use any of them. They had to do a ritual together, and there was enough negative energy in the room already.

"I'm thinking he was worried something like this might happen," Richard said. "He had to deal with some pretty rough characters in his work."

"And now so do we," Della said with a sigh. "So, what's this ritual we have to do?"

Lucas looked at her appreciatively. While she might hate being here, and certainly had a strong dislike for some of the present company, she was ready to do her bit.

That didn't surprise him, but it did make Lucas wonder what was going on in Della's head. In the time since they had foiled Autumn's kidnapping and defeated the sorcerer who had been responsible, Della hadn't spoken a word about anything related to magic. As for the times they had been through together, she had spoken of them only incidentally, through offhand remarks during her darker moods. Yet he knew for a fact that Aunt Mary had been lending Della books about the occult. Those had been returned promptly—fully read, he assumed— and been replaced with further volumes. It seemed that his friend was of two minds, studying a subject she wasn't truly willing to give a part of her life to.

A bit like him, minus the study.

Sadly, that was going to have to change. This was the third serious supernatural incident he and his friends had been involved with in less than six months. He didn't have to be psychic to know that it would not be the last.

"The ritual is quite simple," Richard explained to Della. "We'll walk you through it."

Lucas helped him clear off an area in the middle of the living room, moving the coffee table to one side and clearing a stack of books off a side table next to one of the armchairs. Richard set up a white candle on the side table, circling it with yellow powder while muttering an incantation under his breath. Lucas had seen this ritual preparation before. The light was to provide a metaphysical counterpoint to the darkness they'd be peering into. The circle of specially mixed and blessed powder would act as a protection against anyone or anything blowing the candle out.

After Richard finished preparing the candle, he went upstairs and returned with a tarpaulin that he spread out on the living room floor. He had Della and Lucas stand at the center. Lucas told Della to keep still but otherwise had nothing to do while Richard and Cassandra went to each corner of the tarp, chanting in what Lucas recognized as Medieval Latin. It was one of those languages he was supposed to know and didn't.

He glanced at Della. She looked tense and uncomfortable. At least she wasn't mocking anymore. She'd seen too much to indulge in that when there was work to be done.

Lucas wondered how much of the Latin she understood and decided not to ask. Even if she caught all the words, the content wouldn't make much sense to her. Spells rarely made any sense from a logical point of view. It was a form of knowing and of manipulating the world, beyond logic.

Cassandra moved to the windows and drew all the curtains, then turned off the lights as Richard continued to chant. The room grew dark save for the candlelight and a bit of sunlight filtering around the curtains and from the other rooms. Not pitch black, but dark enough to make a spirit comfortable.

Richard and Cassandra stepped to the center of the tarp, Richard continuing with the chant as Cassandra took the bottle of yellow powder and drew a circle around the four of them. Once finished, Richard stopped chanting.

Lucas could feel the prickle of magic around him. The circle was complete.

"Della," he said. "You need to—"

"Stay within the circle. I know." The way she said it, he knew she wouldn't dare step out of it.

Richard spoke in a low voice. "This is not a summoning. This is a call. The powder is a ward, but it's also an attractant. It will draw in spirits but not let them pass. Those spirits that have already been through this house will most easily move from the Beyond and come into our plane of existence. I'm hoping the thing that came last night will come again."

Della took in a sharp breath. Lucas felt his heart race. Seeing the marks that thing had left behind had been frightening enough, and now Richard wanted to stare at it face-to-face?

He eyed the figure on the wall and then the circle Richard had made around them. Not all magical circles were effective against all spirits and demons. He hoped Richard knew what he was doing.

"Now what?" Della asked.

"We're all going to close our eyes and focus," Richard said. "Try to open your mind to unseen influences. If we have an open attitude, it will help attract the spirits."

"If our eyes are closed, how will we know they've shown up?" Della asked.

"You'll know," Cassandra said with a chuckle.

Lucas closed his eyes, took a deep breath, and tried to relax.

For a long time, nothing happened. Lucas felt no strange sensations, and the only sound he heard was the regular breathing of his friends.

This was typical of rituals. It took time for the mind to settle, for the energies of the ritual to sink in on the spiritual plane. And spirits had their own sense of time. They did not keep to human schedules.

He found himself thinking of Montague. He hadn't known him all that well—the chap had been more Richard's friend than his—but he had known him well enough. Aunt Mary occasionally sent Lucas down to purchase books from him—one of her ways of trying to get him into occult circles. While the fellow had been a bit of a nutter, he had always been friendly enough in his awkward way and up for a pint after any business had been finished. It had been a shock when he had gotten killed. Standing here in his living room trying to summon an intrusive spirit felt almost surreal.

And then suddenly Lucas wasn't imagining Montague anymore; he was seeing him.

Seeing might not have been the best word, more like a vivid image in his mind, a waking dream in which Montague stood out clearly, his tall, bony frame standing in the darkness of Lucas's closed eyes and looking at him inquisitively.

"What are you doing here?" Montague asked. Like in a dream, the words were more imagined than heard. He sounded confused.

"Where?" Della asked.

So she saw him too? Lucas resisted the urge to open his eyes, not wanting to break the thin thread of connection between their consciousness and that of his dead associate who was speaking to them from... somewhere.

Montague looked around, still standing in the darkness that was the only other thing Lucas could see.

"I don't know," the bookdealer whispered.

Lucas had never seen Montague so undone. He had always kept a level head, acting as if he knew exactly what was going on at all times. The fact that he usually did certainly helped with that poise.

But now he seemed utterly at a loss to explain anything.

"Montague," Lucas said, raising his voice slightly and speaking slowly. "Do you remember what happened to you?"

Montague rubbed his forehead. "I... was killed. That just happened a moment ago."

"It's been months," Lucas said.

Montague dropped his hand and stared right at Lucas, who flinched.

"Months? But all the preparations, all the rituals... I must have missed something."

Now Della spoke. "Montague. Some sort of spirit tried to take one of your books. Do you know what it was?"

Montague wasn't listening. He was shaking his head, not looking their way but down, as if deep in thought.

"I must have missed something... missed something."

He faded away.

"Don't open your eyes," Lucas whispered to Della. "Maybe he'll come back."

Or something else.

But nothing did. They stood there another ten minutes with no results.

Eventually Richard let out a sigh and said, "We might as well give it up for now."

Everyone opened their eyes and looked around. Lucas half expected to see Montague sitting on a chair reading.

Della turned to him. "You heard him too. I saw—"

Lucas held up a hand. "Don't tell me. Write down what you saw and heard. Everything, no matter how trivial it might seem. I'll do the same, and we'll compare notes."

Richard broke the circle, and as he and Cassandra cleaned up, Lucas and Della got to work.

Their accounts agreed in every detail.

Della bit her lower lip as she read Lucas's account, growing pale. Once she had finished, she handed the paper back without a word.

Lucas left her on the sofa and went over to where Richard and Cassandra were finishing the cleaning up.

"I take it neither of you saw or heard anything?"

Both shook their heads.

Richard frowned. "It's strange. He entrusted me with his will, and I've been in and out of this house dozens of times since he passed, and yet he hasn't tried to get in touch."

Cassandra studied Lucas for a moment. "It is

strange that he'd pick you—" Then she gestured at Della. "And her."

"I don't have an explanation for it either," Lucas said.

He and Richard went over to where Della was still sitting. She was on her phone.

"You're not getting calls from your professors anxious about your absence already?" Lucas asked.

"No, I'm looking for a hotel. Being from here, you probably don't realize how hard it is to get a room in London on short notice."

For a moment, Lucas was puzzled. Then it came to him.

Oh, you got over your denial about the unseen world, but you're still in denial about your involvement in this.

It was Richard who burst her bubble, and for that, Lucas was grateful. He didn't want the responsibility.

"Darling, you don't need a hotel. You're staying here tonight."

Della looked up from her phone with a mixture of confusion and horror.

Richard continued. "We need your help in case the spirit returns."

3

DETECTIVE CHIEF INSPECTOR Matthews almost had them. Ever since the Oxford affair, where he'd ended up with several dead bodies in his jurisdiction, he had been quietly and systematically assembling evidence against Lucas Lancaster, Richard Camilo, and Della Marshal.

Those three had been up to their necks in illegality all through the summer, and now it looked like they planned to continue into the autumn. First, they had been involved in the Dr. Olding case. Initially it had appeared that Della Marshal and her friends were the victims, but then they were involved in Autumn Birgit Saxe-Coburg's kidnapping. Not as the kidnappers, of course, but Autumn was a known associate of Richard Camilo and Lucas Lancaster. It wasn't hard to link them to the case, especially when they showed up on CCTV breaking into Highgate Cemetery and a nearby pub. Granted, the information those three had given him had led to Ms. Saxe-Coburg's release and the death of a wanted terrorist, but DCI Matthews did not look upon the two occultists and their new American friend as heroes, even if he had released them.

Heroes didn't leave so much chaos in their wake.

He'd learned enough about England's occult circles in the past few months to know they were made up of several rival factions, and some of those factions thought nothing of kidnapping and murdering to advance their power over the others.

Mr. Camilo and Mr. Lancaster simply comprised one of those factions, and they seemed to have roped in Della Marshal, a recent arrival to Oxford University. He still wasn't sure if she had been duped into all this or had been an occultist back in America and in communication with them on the dark web. It didn't matter. She was certainly up to her ears in it now. Those three seemed to be at the center of all the trouble, which meant that they were almost certainly guilty of at least some of it.

The occultism scene wasn't so different than the drugs scene or the illegal gambling scene. If you spent your time with those sorts of characters, it was more than likely that you were a perpetrator as well.

All he had to do was prove it.

He had a mountain of evidence of criminal wrongdoing, enough to have them up on a number of charges, but he preferred to give them their freedom for the time being in order to lure them into revealing their intentions and other criminals in England's occult community.

Then he could charge them with something serious enough to put them away properly. Sentencing in the UK was notoriously soft, and he wanted them to do a good stretch in one of Her Majesty's prisons.

And now he had a new potential ally.

Sebastian Davies sat slumped in the interrogation room in the basement of Oxford's central police station, his nervousness cutting through his drug-induced haze. DCI Matthews already had a file on Mr. Davies, not because he had been previously in trouble with the law—he hadn't—but because his research told him he had been in a relationship with Della Marshal and was at least an acquaintance of Richard Camilo's.

Mr. Davies was a graduate student in the Classics department at Oxford. A rather short, unassuming fellow with black hair and brown eyes, he had a whiff of wealth about him, like most Oxford students. Had a whiff of booze about him too. Not that *that* was such a surprise on a Friday night, but when he had been stopped outside The Knight Errant for a drunk and disorderly charge, the arresting officer had taken one look at his eyes and used a mouth swab to perform an on-the-spot drug test.

Sebastian Davies had tested positive for cocaine.

As soon as he'd been hauled in, DCI Matthews had recognized him, thanked the arresting officer, and taken over the case for himself.

What a stroke of luck! He had Della Marshal's soft spot locked in his interrogation room.

Except one thing made him wonder. The Knight Errant was a gay bar. What was he doing in there?

After letting Mr. Davies stew alone under the harsh lights for a while, the police inspector entered, bringing him a cup of coffee. Had to perk this fellow up, cut through the fog a bit so he could put the screws to him.

In his other hand, he held a folder.

The suspect took the coffee with obvious gratitude and eyed the folder with equally obvious nervousness.

"As I informed you, Mr. Davies, the field tests are initial tests. The ones that really matter are the tests we do back here at the station. They're more accurate."

"One must uphold scientific accuracy," Mr. Davies mumbled into his coffee. He took a sip and made a face. "Ugh. This coffee might just count as police brutality."

"Yes, the coffee here is truly awful," DCI Matthews conceded. "But what you should be more concerned with is your drugs test."

That got his attention.

"Positive for cocaine and GBH," the police officer informed him.

Mr. Davies's eyes widened. "GBH? I didn't take any..." Some memory triggered, and his face fell. "Oh."

"Did you buy the drugs at The Knight Errant?"

"No," the suspect replied, too quickly to be convincing. "I bought them... on the street. I don't know from whom."

DCI Matthews shook his head. Drunk and drugged out of his mind, and yet he remembered to use "whom" instead of "who." These university toffs were insufferable!

He also remembered how to dodge the question effectively. It didn't matter.

"These are very serious charges."

Mr. Davies looked contrite. He also looked bloody nervous. First-time arrestees always did. That could be useful.

"I know." He nodded. "I was a right idiot."

DCI Matthews acted on a hunch.

"We all make mistakes, and from your lack of a record, it appears you don't make many of them. I wouldn't want this to get in the police pages."

Mr. Davies jerked, spilling a bit of his coffee on the table. His eyes went wide, and he looked at the policeman with the face of a trapped animal.

DCI Matthews had guessed correctly. The police pages in the *Oxford Daily Mail* gave the names and arresting locations of those who had been arrested. It also went on the paper's website. Mummy and Daddy might read it and find out he was snorting lines in the bathroom of a gay pub.

Briefly, DCI Matthews felt guilty. He had nothing against the gays. Bloody awful music, but otherwise, they were all right. He knew one or two on the force. But he had a sense that Mr. Davies was not entirely comfortable with his sexuality and that it was probably a new thing to him considering that he had been dating Della Marshal as recently as three months ago.

And that was his hook.

The suspect hadn't said anything. He looked too stunned to speak. DCI Matthews waited. He had all night.

"I..." Mr. Davies started but didn't know how to finish. After a moment he said, "I don't want that either. Is that really necessary? Is there some sort of special fine I could pay?"

"Special fine?"

Mr. Davies rolled his eyes. "You know."

Is this idiot trying to bribe me?

"No, there is no special fine. There is a court date and most likely a fine—just a fine, not a special fine, whatever that is—and most likely some community service and mandatory drug counseling."

"But surely there must be—"

"No."

If he didn't need this chap, he'd have him up on charges of trying to bribe a police officer. That could get him a year.

But DCI Matthews had better uses for him.

The officer decided to go in guns blazing. "Did one of your friends give you the drugs?"

Mr. Davies shifted in his seat, suddenly cagey. "No. As I told you, it was some chap on the street."

"Did Della Marshal give you the drugs?"

The name was like a slap across the face. Mr. Davies gaped at him a moment.

"Della? Why are you bringing her up? She has nothing to do with this."

"That was quite a business you were involved in this summer. That maniac breaking into her flat."

Mr. Davies shuddered. He gulped his coffee and made a face.

"Yes. An... intruder."

The police officer felt a chill go through his body. He remembered back to the tunnels beneath King's Cross station in London. A hazy cloud that formed into figures. For a moment, he swore he had seen Celtic warriors wielding swords and axes.

Then the vision had disappeared, and he had doubted his own eyes, doubted his own sanity.

He couldn't doubt the sword and axe wounds on the victim's body, though.

Murdered by unknown assailants.

That had been the verdict. Mr. Lancaster had told him his theory. It had been too daft to consider. Insane, even.

But he had no other explanation.

The drugged-out, unhappy man slumped in front of him had no other explanation either.

DCI Matthews wanted to change that. He wanted to know what was really going on. And when he knew, he was going to stamp it out.

He leaned forward. Mr. Davies eyed him nervously. It always amazed him how a suspect's fear impulse could sober them up. Worked every time.

"Your ex-girlfriend is in trouble. I don't know what happened between you two, and that's not really pertinent to the case. I'm afraid she's gotten in over her head. I think she's involved in things she doesn't really understand."

Sebastian Davies looked down at the table, his finger tracing a wet path through the little puddle of spilled coffee.

"I made a mess of it."

"A mess of what?" the policeman asked in a fatherly voice. He was old enough to be this university lad's father, although he had no fatherly feeling toward him.

"I didn't figure it out," Mr. Davies said with a helpless gesture. "Not soon enough, in any case. It wasn't fair to start dating her. Not when I was still thinking things through."

DCI Matthews tried to keep his patience. He

wasn't interested in hearing some confession about this man's inadequacy as a boyfriend.

"Tell me more about the attack at the flat. You said that it was a pair of human attackers, dressed in black. But you and I both know that wasn't the case, was it?"

There came that shudder again. Mr. Davies looked at him, pleadingly.

"I told you everything I know. I made a statement."

"Yes, yes. You told me everything you *knew*. But you didn't tell me what you *think*. What you suspect. I've... seen some things too. With Della. It was in London..."

DCI Matthews's voice trailed off. Suddenly, he was at a loss for words too.

Sebastian Davies balled his hands into fists.

"I'm not sure what I saw," he said, his voice an almost inaudible whisper.

"Tell me what you think you saw."

"The night she got attacked in her flat, I went to see her. We'd broken up, had a row."

"About what?"

"Does it matter?"

"About what?" DCI Matthews said in a sterner voice.

Sebastian Davies wilted. "She had gone with Richard and Lucas to The Knight Errant. Richard is a fixture there. I happened to be there, and Della spotted me."

"You two were still dating at the time?"

The deep crimson that came to Mr. Davies's face was all the answer he needed. DCI Matthews went on. "So you went to Ms. Marshal's flat to smooth things over.

Then what happened?"

The suspect made a helpless gesture. "I already gave a statement."

"You left some things out." DCI Matthews waited until Mr. Davies looked at him. "Important things. Things you didn't think we'd believe."

Mr. Davies looked back down at his hands.

"I went up the stairs and heard a commotion inside. I still had my set of keys, so I entered the flat and saw Della fighting two... figures."

"Figures?"

Mr. Davies shook his head. "I was caught by surprise. It was dark except for the light coming in from outside, and I took a knock to the head. I'm not sure what I saw."

"Go on."

"One looked like an old woman, the nastiest

piece of work you have ever seen in your life. The other was a man, a huge man, with a big hammer like the old-time blacksmiths used to use. But there was something strange about them. They didn't seem quite... solid. Felt solid enough when they hit me, though. I can't remember much, only that they rushed me and I shouted something. I don't recall what. No doubt a cowardly squawk of some sort or other. They backed off for a moment and then rushed me again. I was knocked down and got this gash on my forehead."

Mr. Davies raised up his bangs to reveal a fresh scar near the hairline.

DCI Matthews nodded. When they had arrived, they had found the flat in shambles, with broken furniture and a smashed window. They had also found Ms. Marshal holding a blood-soaked washcloth to Mr. Davies's forehead.

But that was not all they had found. They had found Dr. Patricia Olding of the Oxford University Department of Archaeology at the bottom of the stairs, her neck snapped.

"And it was after those two... figures... fled that Dr. Olding showed up and tried to stab the both of you?" DCI Matthews asked.

Mr. Davies nodded.

"She looked normal?"

"Well, if you consider a knife-wielding maniac to be normal."

"But she wasn't indistinct like the other figures."

Mr. Davies didn't look like he wanted to answer that question.

"The first two figures looked a bit like... ghosts."

"I know," DCI Matthews said. "I saw something like that, too, when Ms. Marshal and her friends got into a scrape with some occultists under King's Cross a couple of months ago."

His prisoner looked confused. "I'm sorry, what?"

"She didn't tell you?"

"She hasn't told me much of anything lately. Shortly after that whole dreadful affair, we had a make-up dinner. Strictly platonic, and despite our best efforts at being friends, the evening felt rather distant. That was the last social call. After that, she grew a bit uncommunicative, and I must say that I was getting too involved with my own life to notice much. I mean my new one. The last time I heard from her was to arrange a meeting to retrieve her keys. Even then she had me drop them off with a mutual friend."

"Do you think she'd be open to another meeting?"

Mr. Davies grew guarded. "If I asked nicely, I suppose."

"Don't worry, Mr. Davies. I don't want you to be a sneak. I'm trying to help her. I think she's gotten into a bad crowd."

Or she's leading a bad crowd.

"Richard approached me once or twice at The Knight Errant," Mr. Davies said. "At first I thought he was trying to chat me up, but then he started talking about occultism. Very strange."

That caught DCI Matthews's interest. "Really? What did he say?"

"Not much. I cut him off. I think he wanted me to go to some sort of meeting."

Well, well, well...

"And you said no?"

"He didn't get a chance to ask properly. As soon as I saw where the conversation was headed, I left. I've never been interested in such things. The whole affair with Dr. Olding and that cult cured me of ever changing my mind. And the scene at Della's flat..."

DCI Matthews felt a prick of sympathy. All this fellow wanted to do was sort himself out.

Well, that would have to wait. Some toff's sexual awakening was far less important than figuring out why Della and her friends were in the habit of leaving a trail of corpses in their wake.

"I'd like to help, Mr. Davies. I'd like to keep your name out of the papers. Considering this is your first offense, I'm sure we can get you off with a warning."

"I don't usually use drugs. It was just that I was having such a good night and people were so welcoming and—"

DCI Matthews held up a silencing hand. He had heard it all before. "Oh, I've never done this before," blah, blah, blah. Oddly, this was the first time in his police career where he actually believed it. Again, he felt sorry for this fellow, but he would feel far sorrier if more people died because of Della Marshal, Lucas Lancaster, and Richard Camilo.

"I'll get you off the charges with a warning, Mr. Davies, but you need to do your part. This is what you're going to do. You're going to call up your ex-girlfriend and make nice. Be apologetic—"

"I've already been apologetic."

"Be more apologetic. Say you miss her. Say you want to remain friends. Women love that. See if you can meet with her socially once or twice. Find out what she's up to."

"Up to?"

"With her occultist friends. Lucas Lancaster is

into it as deeply as Richard Camilo. Oh, and if Mr. Camilo invites you to a meeting, I want you to say yes and call me immediately."

"I don't want to spy on—"

"You're helping Della. Mr. Camilo has a list of prior offenses as long as your arm. We have less on Mr. Lancaster, but he's Mr. Camilo's known associate. Those two are dangerous, and they are up to something."

Mr. Davies's gaze flicked to his, showing concern. "Up to something?"

"They are deep in some very dark occult circles. I cannot give you the full particulars of the London case, but I presume you heard about the death of Einhardt Donner at King's Cross?"

"The terrorist? Wait, they were mixed up in that?"

DCI Matthews nodded.

Mr. Davies sputtered. "B-but why are they still free?"

"Lack of evidence. They came out looking more like victims than perpetrators, but I know for a fact that they were at least partially involved with that set. I just need to prove it. You can help, but you mustn't rush in. Move slowly so as to gain their confidence. They might be dangerous."

The suspect was fully sober now. Amazing how that worked. "We have to save Della."

"We do." *Save her for a prison sentence, more like.*

Mr. Davies looked him in the eye again. "I'll do whatever you want."

4

A NOISE WOKE HER, sending Della's heart to racing and making her sit bolt upright in bed.

She stared into the near-pitch darkness, just the faintest stream of feeble streetlight reaching around the edges of the blinds to cast a dim glow across the room, more shadow than substance.

The house was silent. Whatever the sound had been—and all she knew was that a sound had woken her, something sudden, something unusual—it did not repeat.

Della threw on a nightgown and slippers and moved as quietly as she could to the door, pressing her ear against the wood to listen.

She caught the faint sound of snoring from one of the other rooms. It must have been Richard, because he had taken the upstairs room, and Lucas was on the sofa in the back room downstairs.

No, she thought. *No way am I going to walk through a haunted house alone at night.*

She felt tempted to turn on a light, although if someone or something was moving around, that would signal her presence.

Whoosh!

The sound made her jerk back from the door.

What had that been? It sounded like a sudden rush of air, although she hadn't felt anything from the crack beneath the door.

Her skin prickled. Her hand went to the doorknob and paused.

The faintest noise came to her ears, tickling her senses at the very limits of her hearing. She couldn't be sure what it was. A hint of movement, perhaps.

She eased open the door...

...and immediately regretted it.

The stairwell was illuminated with a flickering yellowish-orange light, like faint firelight, yet she smelled no fire and felt no heat.

She heard something, though.

It was a soft crackling, mixed in with what sounded like rushing air. The sound was soft, barely registering on her hearing. It was this that she had heard from the other side of her door.

A door she seriously regretted having opened.

The light grew stronger, and she got the impression of movement and a steady brightening. The source of that light was ascending the steps.

Fear clenched her throat. Her entire body trembled. Despite wanting to run shrieking back into her bed to hide under the covers, she stood rooted to the spot, watching in horrified fascination as the glow grew brighter.

And then the figure appeared.

It was not as she had imagined it earlier in the day. She had thought of some flaming man, like a special effect in some cheap action movie where the bad guy caught on fire and turned into a human torch.

The sight that confronted her was far more surreal.

There was fire, yes. There was a figure, yes. But the two did not add up into a coherent whole.

What came up the stairs and turned toward her was a fiery figure made up not of flames but of lines of fire, thin lines like the squiggles of some demon child's drawing. These lines made up a squat figure only a little taller than Della. The lines flared and dimmed like actual flames but never went out. The pulsing, constantly changing light of the countless lines that made up the spirit hypnotized her. She stared, fascinated more than frightened, as the thing approached her.

Only now, as it drew close, did she feel the heat. Only now did she smell the brimstone.

Della glanced at the carpeted floor, expecting to see smoldering footsteps that would soon flare up and set the whole house on fire, but she saw no such thing. There was no trace of the spirit's passing.

It can burn when it wants to, though.

Step by step it approached her, the faintest crackling the only sound it made.

Where are the others? Did it already kill Lucas downstairs?

She glanced at Richard's bedroom door. It remained closed. Cassandra would be no help either. She had gone home.

It's up to me, she realized. *Why is it always up to the least experienced person here?*

The creature was almost within reach now.

Della shook herself out of her fear, summoned her will and shouted, "Begone! Begone! Three times I command you, Begone!"

The spirit stopped. Della got the odd impression

that it cocked its head and looked on her with amusement.

Della took a step back. That simple charm had worked on ghosts and water spirits. Why wasn't it working now?

The thing swiped an arm at her, its limb flaring up in midswing.

Della's fencing training kicked in, and she dodged back, leaning backward to get even more distance.

Instead of hitting her head, the fiery arm hit the doorframe, leaving a smoldering mark.

Richard's door burst open. Dressed only in his underwear, he held out a brass amulet in his hand and shouted a string of incomprehensible words. Della had no idea what language it was, or indeed if it was a language.

It did have an effect, though. The spirit whirled around.

Flaring up both arms, it rushed for Richard.

"No!" Della shouted.

Richard called out another enchantment, holding his ground and keeping the amulet in front of him.

The flaming figure stopped in its tracks. Lucas came thundering up the stairs.

He stopped dead at the top of the stairs, jaw dropping.

The figure crumpled in on itself, legs folding up, head and shoulders hunching down until it turned into a fireball the size of basketball.

It shot right at Lucas.

Lucas ducked, and the ball of flames hit the wall inches above his head and vanished, leaving a smoking patch in the wallpaper.

For a second, everyone stood there, stunned.

Until a tongue of flame licking up from the blackened circle urged them to action.

Della ran back into her room to get the glass of water sitting by her bed. Lucas ran to the bathroom, no doubt intending on grabbing the glass by the sink.

Richard calmly ducked behind his bedroom door and came out with a fire extinguisher. He gave a burst to the patch then went over and sprayed Della's doorframe. Della and Lucas stood there dumbly, each holding a glass.

"Tsk, tsk, you really need to get a bit more Johnny-on-the-spot if you're going to keep up with me," Richard said.

Now that she could concentrate on something other than dying, Della realized he was only wearing his underwear.

Black silk underwear slightly more revealing than the average pair of Speedos.

"Um, could you put something on, please?"

Richard looked at her curiously. "What's the matter?"

"While I'm grateful that you saved us from being burned to death by some weird hell creature, I don't really want to see you in a banana hammock."

"I second the motion," Lucas said.

"Oh, very well. Lucas, go check that everything's all right downstairs."

Della returned to her room to get changed. Her clock said 3:30 a.m. She doubted if any of them would get any more sleep that night.

She had barely pulled up her jeans when Lucas came thundering back up the stairs.

"That stack of books is gone!" he shouted.

She hurried to get her shirt on and flung open the door, just as Richard came out of his own room, thankfully more dressed this time.

"No, they're not. I brought them up here with me. Pleasant bedtime reading. I put a warding circle around them before turning in. That's why the creature came up here, I suppose. To have a second go at them."

"You could have told us," Lucas grumbled.

Richard shrugged. "I don't see why it makes much difference. What I don't understand is why my other ward didn't work. I put an enchantment on the house to wake me up if a spirit manifested."

"I don't know why I didn't wake up when it came through the wall again," Lucas said. "Oh, there's another man-shaped burn mark on your living room wall."

"Oh dear. How am I ever going to sell this place? You know, it took a lot for me to wake up. I didn't until Della tried to banish the thing."

Lucas turned to her. "It sounds like we had some sort of spell put on us so we remained asleep. How did you wake up so easily?"

"I'm not sure," Della admitted. "I heard a sound and woke up."

"So whatever spell our unknown friend cast on us didn't work on you," Richard said. "My, my, you are just full of surprises."

Della let out a long, slow sigh. Great. Here she was being special again. She had spent her entire life being overlooked, and now she was the center of some very bad attention. She knew enough about magic to know that the person who cast that spell on them would figure out it hadn't worked on her. That would make her the target of a stronger spell next time.

And there would most certainly be a next time.

"I'm going to make some tea," Della said.

Richard turned to Lucas with a smile. "She gets more and more English every day."

5

"I'VE BEEN STUDYING the stack of books the fire spirit tried to steal on its first visit," Richard said over an early breakfast an hour later.

"Have you found any clue as to why it wanted those particular volumes?" Lucas asked.

Richard considered a moment, pushing around his scrambled eggs with his fork. "I'm not sure. There were five books in that stack, all from the seventeenth or eighteenth centuries and all roughly on a similar subject. I'm beginning to get an inkling of Montague's bizarre filing system. He organized by theme. Well, in a manner of speaking. For example, he wouldn't organize by author or general subject or publisher or any of the other criteria rare bookdealers use, at least the sane ones. But when you start to look at what is bunched with what, you get a sort of feel for why certain books are clumped together. Since the books on the protected table are the rarest volumes from that purchase in Orkney, I've gotten a small-scale look into Montague's filing system. Far easier to understand than plucking sense out of the vast chaos that is this house."

"And what did you find?" Lucas asked. He was beginning to suspect his friend got as much enjoyment out of unraveling the puzzle of Montague's mind as he did looking through the books themselves. Richard had always been a bit of a student of human character. Hanging out at The Knight Errant, he'd had plenty of opportunity to indulge that side of his nature.

"All the books are from the worst period of witch executions in Scotland, and all were written in Scotland by Scots. That's rare right from the start. We have few works from the Scottish Masters from this period. While the witchcraft trials were beginning to fade in England, witch hunts in Scotland were still in full swing. It was an extremely dangerous time to write about occultism in the north."

"How did they get away with it?" Lucas asked.

"They all used pen names, but later research has

identified them. Sadly, in a couple of cases, they were caught and named in court records."

Lucas felt a chill. Richard didn't need to tell him how those trials had ended.

If we had been born at a different time, it might have been us burning at the stake.

"So what do the books cover?" Della asked.

"Various subjects. In those days, most magical grimoires were sort of catch-all collections of spells, gazetteers of sacred sites and demons, how-to guides for making amulets—pretty much anything you can think of related to magic. Books were rare, especially these books, and you might only get your hands on one every few years. Each book had to give the reader a wide range of things to study."

"I've noticed they're all pretty thick," Lucas said.

"Indeed they are. But flipping through them, I found they all cover one subject in common, an unusual subject you don't see much written about. It's a ward of sorts, a protection against the ley lines."

"Why would you need that?" Della asked.

"As you know, the ley lines are powerful earth energy. They can be used for good or harm, but they are themselves neutral. A bit like a hammer. You can use it to make one of those lovely chairs Lucas is so good at crafting, or you can bash someone's head in. The ley lines have another aspect to them, however, a sort of defense system for the network."

"Whatever for?" Lucas asked.

Richard studied him for a moment and shook his head. "You grow up with one of the most accomplished practitioners of the Craft and you have to ask that?"

Lucas looked away. He didn't want to have anything to do with this at all. Even Della could be more accepting of taking on this role. She had spent the first twenty-five years of her life in blissful ignorance. He had learned the darker nature of the occult at all too young of an age.

Twenty years ago on All Hallows' Eve... a dark figure emerges from his bedroom wall... nine-year-old Lucas screams and clutches the sheets... his parents rush in, chanting wards and counterspells.

They are not strong enough. Two of the greatest occultists of their generation are not strong enough.

And they vanish. Absorbed into the wall with that creature.

Lucas let out a little shudder and forced himself to pay attention as Richard continued.

"Like any magic, or indeed any power, including living things, ley magic has natural self-defense mechanisms. If something tries to disrupt the leys or destroy them, they will fight back."

"Wait a minute," Della said. "I thought leys were the magic of this whole planet. Aren't they supposed to be a network of the earth's power?"

Richard smiled. "Right you are, girlie. Looks like you've been studying more than your friend here."

"Then how can they be disrupted?" she asked. "One of Aunt Mary's books said that massive modern constructions, even strip mines, haven't been able to disturb the ley lines. People have been able to tap into their power and even change their nature a bit, but not stop the network or destroy it."

"Mundane human affairs can't touch the ley lines, you're correct. But there are some types of magic that can interfere with their power and kick off what you might think of as an immune response."

"Like what? Do the books say?"

"Sadly, no. That's not what these books concern themselves with. They only hint at it. What they do talk about is a form of protection when the ley lines strike back. Certain magical wards and protective circles that will keep you from suffering the effects."

"And what effects would those be?" Lucas asked.

"Destruction of all intelligent life on the planet. Wiping the slate clean, so to speak."

Silence fell in the room as everyone let that soak in.

"So..." Lucas started, not quite sure how to finish. "How would this manifest?"

"Unclear. It's never happened before. At least not on a large scale. There are signs that it has happened on a localized basis, however. It might explain some ancient mysteries. The disappearance of the Anasazi, for example. Or the sudden collapse of the Indus civilization."

"Now wait a minute!" Della jabbed a finger at him. "There's good evidence that the Anasazi suffered an extended drought and had to leave their pueblos to find a better place to live. The same thing might have happened with the Indus civilization. There's no evidence that they disappeared overnight. I've read about those sites. If you look at the dwellings, you don't see everything in place. The buildings got cleared out. They're not like Pompeii."

"Ah, ever the archaeologist! Perhaps you're right, but how about this? In the late nineteenth century, a group of wealthy English occultists and their servants moved to a remote part of Yorkshire. They bought a village from the locals and evicted the previous residents. They wanted a place of their own where they could cast their magic undisturbed by outsiders, especially the authorities. This was near Pendle Hill, the center of the Pendle Witch trials back in the seventeenth century. The village had a menhir, a Neolithic standing stone, right on the village green. That's probably why they chose it. All went quietly for a time, although other occultists noted some disturbances in the ley lines. Several contemporary practitioners wrote about it."

"In some nonsense magazine?" Della said.

"No. Private letters and diaries. This isn't the sort of thing to write about for public consumption. Anyway, one night there was a large pulse along the ley lines. You didn't have to be a Sensitive to feel it. It led to several cases of madness among the mundane population and even a few earth tremors. Mainstream science had no explanation for it and so quickly forgot the matter. It was remembered in Yorkshire, however."

"How so?" Lucas asked.

"Wait. You don't know this story? Goodness, Lucas, I'm sure Aunt Mary has told you this. You need to start paying more attention. It was remembered because everyone in that village vanished. The first person to notice was the postman, naturally enough. He called the authorities, and they came in. Not a trace of any of the fifty-odd people who had been living there. The occultists, their servants, all gone. There are some reports that they found a large circle of ash around the menhir in the village green. Some theorize that the residents were performing a ritual when the ley lines decided to get rid of them."

"You talk of the ley lines as if they were intelligent," Della said. "None of my reading indicates that."

Richard shook his head. "They aren't. Think of it like your immune system. Your white blood cells don't actually think about fighting bacteria, they just automatically do it. On a larger scale, you don't think about pulling your hand away from something that's unexpectedly hot. It's a natural instinct. All living things have a survival instinct. The ley lines are no different."

"So they're alive?"

"If you expand your definition of life, yes."

Lucas shifted in his seat. He had experienced an increasing awareness of the ley energy as he grew older. Aunt Mary had said that her own power was diminishing, that it was being passed onto him as it had always passed from generation to generation in his family since before recorded history. Lucas had learned to feel the changes and pulses in ley energy, especially with the turning of the seasons or from their interaction with various rituals. But he had never suspected ley lines could be actively dangerous.

"So now what?" Della asked. Lucas would like to know that too.

"I suggest you two go up and speak with Aunt Mary about this. She might have some answers. I'll come join you once I get through a few things here."

"We shouldn't leave you alone with that fire creature," Lucas said.

"It failed twice. I suspect whoever sent it will change tactics. Perhaps a good, old-fashioned break-in. That would be dangerous in this neighborhood, but he or she or they might get desperate."

"I don't understand why they would want this sort of magic," Lucas said. "I haven't felt any changes in the ley lines recently. Certainly nothing that would hint at a massive catastrophe."

"Maybe they know something we don't," Della said.

Lucas bit his lip. Considering how powerful the magic must have been to summon a creature like they had seen, their opponents probably knew a lot they didn't.

A couple of hours later, riding the Oxford Tube bus line back home, they got a new surprise.

Della's phone rang. She checked it and raised an eyebrow.

"It's Sebastian."

Lucas tried to ignore the spike of inexplicable jealousy he felt and asked as casually as he could, "What could he want?"

"I have no idea. We haven't spoken in weeks."

Della answered the call. Lucas looked out the window at the rolling fields and other lanes of early morning traffic and pretended not to listen in.

"Hi... Yeah, I'm all right, and you?... I got a full slate of lectures too... Really?... That's good... Yeah, I suppose it's just that—Um, okay... Could we do it tomorrow?... Oh, I see... Yeah, sure..."

This is maddening, Lucas thought. *It's like being cut out of a conversation. Wait, were you ever invited? Perhaps you shouldn't be listening in!*

But he did listen in. He couldn't help it.

"It's all right, really... Of course I meant it... Yes, I still care about you..."

Lucas squirmed. Had Della glanced at him when she said that? Lucas still kept his face turned to the window, but the glass betrayed her. A movement in the faint reflection. Yes, she most definitely looked at him when she said that last bit.

"All right, but not this afternoon. This evening...

The Eagle and Child? Sure. I guess there won't be too many tourists this time of year."

She hung up.

"Did a fiery demon pass through his wall?" Lucas asked. Silly joke, but he wanted to prompt her to talk about the call, to tell him about a conversation that was quite obviously none of his business.

"He just wants to meet up."

"Oh."

She didn't say anything more. Lucas waited, the moment drawing out, the fleeting chance for him to add something to his noncommittal and yet blatantly insecure monosyllable passing. Then the moment passed for Della to respond.

They settled into silence and remained in that state for the hour it took them to make it back to Oxford.

6

THE EAGLE and Child would have been one of Della's favorite Oxford pubs if it wasn't so damn crowded all the time.

The front entrance was flanked by a pair of cozy nooks, perfect for drinking with a date or two or three good friends. A slightly larger room just behind held a couple of larger tables and a fireplace. It was here that the Inklings, a writer's group that included J.R.R. Tolkien, C.S. Lewis, and several lesser-known writers, used to meet back in the 1930s. Because of this, the place was usually swamped with tourists. On a rainy evening in late October, however, only locals and students sat here, with the notable exception of a middle-aged Japanese man, a guidebook open next to his pint, who sat next to the fireplace and looked around him in wide-eyed wonder. Della wondered if he could read the captions on the old photographs hanging on the walls around him.

Della remembered the first time she had come here, the very first day she had moved to Oxford, well before her lectures had started and before she had known anyone. Going alone into a pub was something her shyness had always kept her from doing—she'd heard it felt awkward even for normal people—but her curiosity had gotten the better of her. The place had been packed, and she had ended up tucked in a corner, an unseen wallflower, not far from where that vacationing businessman sat now. She suspected she had stared around her like he had.

The Lord of the Rings, The Chronicles of Narnia, The Silmarillion... all had been discussed in these rooms. Perhaps portions had been read aloud here or ideas for the next chapter scribbled on notepads or napkins. Her childhood love of fantasy fiction seemed to seep through the very walls.

Reading fantasy had been an escape from her lonely and awkward childhood and her even lonelier and more awkward teen years. It had remained a guilty and increasingly secretive pleasure through university and into graduate school.

She still had a stack of unread novels in her

apartment. Ever since magic had turned out to be real, she'd lost interest in getting through them. So many people around her said that reading about wizards and dragons was immature, and now she agreed, if for completely different reasons.

Della sat sipping her pint at the table next to the one occupied by the Japanese man. Getting this seat counted as a minor miracle. Three students had just been leaving as she turned from the bar with her drink, and she had swooped down on their table like a buzzard going for roadkill. A few people passing into the pub gave significant looks to the two lone drinkers occupying tables too large for them before making their way to the more modern and far less atmospheric room in the back. There had been a time, Della mused, not three months ago, when she would have cringed at their gaze. At times even now, her old shy self reemerged. But not today. Not the day after facing a fire demon.

Sebastian came through the front door. Della tensed. Yes, now was a perfectly legitimate time to feel self-conscious. He gave her an awkward smile, mouthed the words "fashionably late," the old joke, and headed to the bar.

He returned a minute later, pint in hand.

"Tsk, tsk," he said. "Taking up an entire table in

the fireplace room. I thought that was a hanging offense."

"It's not regularly enforced."

"Glad to hear it. How are you?" Sebastian asked.

"Excited about the new term." *Terrified of being scorched to a crisp by a demon.*

"I have some excellent lectures this term. I was really lucky to get into Professor Davidson's course on Greek Morals..."

Sebastian rattled on about his lectures, the books he had bought, and a short trip to Greece he had taken while Della had been down in London trying to free a kidnapped member of the royal family. He was his usual witty, charming self, with lots of interesting anecdotes about his travels and his friends and intriguing facts he had gleaned from obscure journals.

It was all very pleasant, and he let her speak too. He had always been good at that, unlike so many guys who just talked right over her. She told him about her lectures, the books she had read, all those pleasant, interesting, and ultimately unimportant things that used to fill up her life. All those things that made up the entirety of the lives of most of the people around her.

It was a normal, intellectually stimulating

conversation between two people, an experience that had somehow escaped her for much of her life. It had always been pretty easy with Sebastian. She'd never had many relationships before, and this had been the best.

At least until he had come out as gay. Or, more accurately, until she had discovered that he had been hiding his sexuality from her.

As the conversation continued, as they talked about everything and nothing, she wanted to blurt out a question about how he was enjoying Oxford's lone gay bar or if he had found a boyfriend yet. But that would have been cruel. Della knew Sebastian felt guilty about hiding it from her, and she couldn't really feel all that angry about being out of the loop when he had been hiding it from himself too. Yet the flow of irrelevant words that passed back and forth between them grew increasingly annoying.

As he started in on the thrill of visiting Delphi just a couple of months before, she couldn't take it anymore.

"How did you command Wayland the Smith and Old Mother Shipton?" she blurted out.

Sebastian's drink stopped halfway to his lips.

"I beg your pardon?"

"That night you came to my apartment and we

got attacked. I was struggling with an old crone and a huge guy dressed as a blacksmith. They were spirits. Folk spirits. When you came in, they rushed at you, and you shouted at them. Stopped them in their tracks. You shouldn't have been able to do that."

"All I recall is that they thumped me over the head and ran off."

His words lacked conviction.

"You know there was more to it than that. We've avoided talking about it ever since that night."

"Della, this is bonkers."

"Is it? You saw them yourself. Did they look normal to you?"

"I admit they looked a bit... blurry, but that was a trick of the light. It was dark, I was taken by surprise and confused, I—"

"Did I look blurry? Did anything else in the room look blurry?"

Sebastian set his glass down and stared into the amber liquid as if he was going to find an answer there.

When he didn't reply, Della went on.

"This is important, Sebastian."

"I've become adept at ignoring important facts," he mumbled.

Della reached out and tousled his soft brown

hair. It had been a while since she had done that. She used to love to. Briefly she wondered why she was doing it now, but she clamped that thought down.

"It's okay. I understand." A flash of irritation in his eyes made her hurry to continue. "I *do* understand. Not about... you know... but about not wanting to face facts. Some really strange things have been happening to me for the past few months, and I need to sort them out. I could use as much help as I can get. You have some things to sort out too."

"Like if I got beaten up by a ghost? Somehow I didn't feel right informing the police. I didn't want to be remanded to a lunatic asylum."

Della pulled her hand back. Was he saying she was crazy?

Sebastian must have read the expression on her face because he hurried to say, "No, I don't think you're off your rocker. I think you're simply overwhelmed. Getting attacked by your professor, that horrible cult, it would be too much for anyone."

"It was too much. Sometimes all I want to do is hide in the library for the next five years. But a lot of this stuff is real, Sebastian. I think you know that."

Her ex-boyfriend's eyes looked at everything except her.

"I don't know. I do know you're in trouble, Della.

I think you've gotten too wrapped up in this stuff. Richard has spoken to me a few times at the pub. You know his reputation?"

Della smiled. "As a party animal? Oh yes. He gave me the worst hangover of my life."

"No, I mean everyone starts humming the *X-Files* theme when he walks in the room. He believes in witchcraft and demons and all sorts of things."

"Some of those things might be true." *All of those things are definitely true.*

"Dr. Olding's cult thought so, and look what they did."

"Richard is different."

"Perhaps. Perhaps not. What if he's just like them and only hides it better? Della, I'd be shattered if anything happened to you. I don't want you to get hurt."

She could have quite easily said something cruel at this point. No one had hurt her as much this year as he had. Instead she held back. It was only natural that he be worried about her considering what they had been through. And if he was in denial, could she really blame him? She had been in denial for a lot longer while faced with a lot more evidence.

"I'm fine," Della lied. "The thing with my advisor just sent me for a loop. I realized that there's a lot more going on in the world than meets the eye. I think you know that too. You neatly sidestepped the whole issue of the crone and the smith being blurry. You know something strange happened."

Sebastian winced. "I don't know what happened."

"Neither do I. Not really. That's what I'm trying to figure out. All I know is that a lot more of this kind of thing is going to happen."

Sebastian glanced around him before leaning in and lowering his voice. "So you're saying there's more of them out there? That Dr. Olding's cult wasn't the only one?"

Della shook her head. When she replied, she kept her voice barely above a whisper. "There are a lot more people practicing the occult than I ever suspected. And they're *serious*, Sebastian. They're in it for power, and they can get it too. You only saw a little bit. And the way you made Old Mother Shipton and Wayland the Smith stop in their tracks, that was amazing. You may have the Talent."

"The what?"

"Magical Talent."

"Oh, come now. You're really going too far."

Della held up a hand. She was going too fast with him. "Just keep an open mind, that's all I ask."

"I'm a little more concerned about these occultists you mentioned than any latent ability I might have at reading tea leaves."

She put a hand on his then withdrew it, worried he might misinterpret the move.

"I could use all the friends I could get right now," she said.

"Well, if it's occultists you're worried about, I'll help. But I need to know more about what's going on. I don't understand any of this."

"Excuse me."

The strange voice cutting into their conversation made them both jump. The Japanese tourist stood next to their table.

Della's heart raced. How much had he heard? Was he one of them?

He held up his phone. "Could you take a picture of me?"

Della almost fainted with relief. Sebastian flashed her an ironic smile, took the phone, and started taking pictures of the man standing next to different spots in the pub.

That night Della curled up in bed under a thick comforter and buried herself in some class reading. She needed to keep up with her university work and get some relaxation while she could. It looked like she wouldn't get to do much of either of those things over the next few days.

Her phone rang. Cursing herself for not putting it on silent, she grabbed it. It was Richard.

"Hello, darling. Have you shacked up with Lucas yet?"

"Very funny. What's up?"

"That's a boldly personal question coming from someone like you. Oh, you mean what's going on? Not much. Lucas invited me to come up tomorrow to have a chat with Aunt Mary. Funny how we all call her "aunt," isn't it? Just seems to fit. Anyway, we're going to burrow through her library like a pack of stoats and see what we come up with. Should be heaps of fun. Want to join us?"

"Do I have a choice?"

"Darling, it is entirely up to you whether you want to save the world."

Della passed a hand over her face, feeling an anxiety attack coming on. She'd held it together the past couple of days through a sense of self-preservation. But now, alone in her flat and talking to a friend who only wanted her to read some books, she felt overwhelmed. It was during these quiet times that she felt the most vulnerable. Perhaps because she had more time to think about what she was headed into. It wouldn't stop with a quiet day reading at Uncle Philip and Aunt Mary's. The information they gleaned from that remarkable library would lead them into more trouble than they had already faced.

Far more.

"All right," she said at last. "Tell Lucas I'll show up at the farmhouse at ten tomorrow morning. Leave me alone until then."

She would read, nestled in her bed. It was her way of refilling the well of her energy, which was already getting pretty empty.

"Righty-ho. Get some beauty sleep, even though you don't need it. Then we'll spend a pleasant day in the country."

Della groaned, hung up, and switched her phone to silent. Tomorrow would be anything but pleasant.

7

"HERE'S SOMETHING INTERESTING," Aunt Mary said, placing her fingertip on a line in an aged tome.

Lucas and Richard looked up from their respective armchairs. All three of them were sitting in Aunt Mary's extensive library of occult books, which was the largest Lucas had ever seen besides Montague's. All the bookcases in the large room were lined with shelves that rose to the high, timbered ceiling. At one end, by the window overlooking the broad front field with its ancient oak, stood an antique table covered in maps, each crisscrossed with ley lines.

They had been at it for hours, and as was typical with occult research, they had been sent down a series of rabbit holes, tracing complex paths of archaic knowledge without finding what they sought.

And as usual, it was Aunt Mary who found the most pertinent information.

"This is about summoning fire spirits," she said, peering through her wire-rimmed spectacles at the old type. "It comes from a Scottish text from 1508, although I'm using the reprint from 1724. There are limits to my book budget." Aunt Mary gave an apologetic smile. "It says that there are several types of fire spirits that can be summoned from Hell."

"There is no Hell," Richard said. "Although parts of Blackpool come close."

"Come now. You know that work this old is often garlanded with Christian trappings. It helped keep the authorities at bay. Now listen to this. Most fire spirits are general spirits that can be summoned from any location. They are of fiery form and burn anything they touch. That doesn't sound like the one you faced. Otherwise, Montague's whole house would have gone up in flames."

Lucas nodded. "This one seemed to be made of fire but was enough in the spirit world that it didn't burn anything except when it first manifested through the wall and when it attacked."

"That's the spirit raising its energy level,"

Richard said. "It had to just to materialize, which is why it burnt the wall, and then it raised it again when it tried to take a swipe at Della. Otherwise, it barely registered on this plane as anything more than light and a bit of brimstone stench."

"There's a type of fire spirit that fits that description," Aunt Mary said. "Actually several. They are the *genius loci* of several ancient sites at certain nexuses of the ley lines. Each of these can only be summoned at that particular site, although they can then be sent to wherever the summoner wishes, to return back to the nexus before returning to the spirit world."

"And where are these sites?" Lucas asked.

"All over. Mostly but not exclusively in volcanic areas. There's one in Iceland, another in Japan, one in Santorini, but mostly importantly, there's one in Orkney."

"Well now," Richard said with a smile. "It seems our friends are being a wee bit too obvious."

"That could be a coincidence," Lucas said. When he saw the looks the two more- experienced occultists gave him, he quickly added, "Or they might be trying to put us off the scent."

"Unlikely," Aunt Mary said, "and here's why. Frederick MacHugh was a recluse. I never met him, and neither did anyone here in England. He didn't even correspond with many people down here. Montague was an exception because he was such a good supplier of books. Frederick MacHugh was very much tied to the magic of his home islands, of which there is more than enough to keep a practitioner busy for a lifetime. From what I hear, on the rare instances when he did engage in group rituals, it was only because more than one person was needed for a ritual he wanted to do, and he only worked with other islanders."

"So they're the only people who would have known what was in his library," Lucas said.

Richard grinned and elbowed Lucas in the ribs. "See, Aunt Mary, he's not so dim-witted after all."

"Very funny. Any idea who might be behind this?" Lucas asked.

Aunt Mary grimaced. "Sadly, no. While the Orcadian practitioners aren't all as reclusive as Frederick MacHugh, they tend to be quite regional. They work within Scotland or preferably only with other islanders. I'm not sure I've ever met one, and I haven't corresponded enough with any of them to get any clues as to who might be behind this. Sadly, I also don't know any of them well enough to trust them with what I know."

"So where was our flaming *genius loci* from?" Richard asked.

Aunt Mary struggled out of her armchair. Lucas watched her with concern. She had been slowing down in recent years. She wasn't up for the long country walks she used to love, and late at night, when she was tired, Lucas noticed a slight tremor in her hands.

Her mind, however, was just as sharp as ever. Lucas couldn't imagine a time when that would not be the case.

She moved over to a shelf beside the table and ran her finger along the spines of a long line of folded maps before selecting the three that covered the Orkney Islands. These she unfolded, covering the table and the scattering of maps already laid out on it. She weighed down each corner with a small piece of jasper. Aunt Mary had explained why she used that particular stone when studying maps, but Lucas had forgotten the reason. He was, he had to admit, a terrible student. Richard or Della would have been better off having her as an aunt. If Lucas could have his way, he would have been raised by a pipefitter and a secretary in Wolverhampton. Dreary place, Wolverhampton, but at least they didn't deal with too many summonings.

The maps were standard Ordnance Survey maps of the island group at the 1:25000 scale, a highly detailed map produced by the government that showed roads, buildings, copses, ferry lanes, currents, and most importantly, historic and ancient sites, of which the islands had plenty.

Located just off the north coast of Scotland, the Orkney island group was made up of several large islands, including the biggest, called "Mainland," in the center. To the south of Mainland was Hoy and South Ronaldsay, and to the north lay Rousay, Shapinsay, Westray, Papa Westray, Eday, Stronsay, Sanday, and North Ronaldsay.

He knew people who loved staring at maps, people who felt a thrill of potential adventure from looking at details of far-off places. Lucas was not one of those people. Give him his workshop, walks in the countryside, and visits to Oxford to see his few but choice friends, and he felt content. Despite having sufficient money to afford a holiday every now and then, he had never been one for travel. He hadn't even been out of the country for the past five years.

Looking at the maps of the Orkney Islands, however, he felt strangely intrigued. The jagged coastlines and their precarious position between the North Sea and the North Atlantic must make them particularly rough in winter. That kind of climate bred a tough and self-reliant people. He wasn't surprised that Frederick MacHugh had been a recluse.

Between the larger islands lay countless smaller ones. And why was North Ronaldsay at the opposite end of the island group from South Ronaldsay? Shouldn't they be closer together? Such strange names, so foreign. He suspected they were a mix of Pictish and Old Norse. He knew both the Picts and the Vikings had settled there and that there had been a thriving culture in the Neolithic. The place was littered with menhirs, stone circles, and other prehistoric monuments.

The three maps were crisscrossed with thin lines made with a fine pen. Aunt Mary had added those. They were ley lines, lines of power along the earth that the ancients had tapped into by building roads and religious centers on them.

And there certainly were a lot of them. Such a dense cluster of ley lines was rare and powerful.

"We should get Della in here to look at this," Lucas said. Richard, standing next to him and studying the map, murmured assent.

"Leave her alone," his aunt replied. She given her a pile of books, and Della had retreated to the kitchen, where they hadn't heard from her for more than two hours.

Lucas didn't understand why she needed to cut herself off so much. He enjoyed his privacy too. After the media frenzy surrounding his parents' disappearance and the occasional reporter still dogging his footsteps to this day, he valued the quiet life. With her it seemed something more, though. It was like she could only deal with people for a certain length of time and then had to retreat into solitude to recharge.

Poor girl, he thought. *She's going to get precious little solitude in the coming days.*

Lucas snapped out of his thoughts as Aunt Mary began to trace the lines with her finger.

"The book mentioned that the *genius loci* for that particular fire spirit comes from Maeshowe. That's right here on the Orkney Mainland. You've probably heard of this particular monument."

"One of the biggest passage graves in Europe," Richard said. "In the main chamber are some Viking runes."

Lucas nodded. The monument was so famous that even he had heard of it. "They were carved by some Norsemen caught in a blizzard, isn't that right?"

"That's right," Aunt Mary said. "On Christmas 1153, in fact. The Earl Harald was leading some of his retainers from the town of Stromness to the parish of Firth when they got caught in a storm. The only thing close by was the grass-covered tumulus over the tomb. They broke in and used it as shelter."

"Things were much freer in those days," Richard said with a smile. "I can't even so much as light a candle in a passage grave without incurring a fine."

"And you've incurred quite a few," Aunt Mary said, chuckling. "The Norsemen, bored during the storm, started carving their names and little messages on the walls of Maeshowe's main chamber. But the Earl Harald knew that this was more than a simple tomb. It was a major center for magic, being at a nexus of ley lines. The passage leading into the main chamber is lit up by the rising sun on midwinter morning, a sign that the seasons are about to shift. Thus it is associated not only with earth energy, but with change and fire."

"I think I see where this is going," Richard said.

Lucas wished Richard would say more, because he didn't see where this was going at all. Listening to these two talk reminded him of the two chaps at the local computer repair shop. He had to bring his laptop in for servicing the previous month, and when those two started gabbling at each other, they might as well have been speaking Swahili for all he understood.

"Exactly. This is the origin of the fire spirit," Aunt Mary said as if it was the most obvious thing in the world. "Apparently the blizzard grew worse and worse, and having no fuel, the Norsemen were in danger of freezing to death. The Earl Harald made the connection between the power center of the nexus and the fire magic he could sense in the area and summoned a fire spirit to heat up the chamber and save their lives. Whether it had been in existence in Neolithic times when Maeshowe was first built is unclear, but after the Earl Harald's visit, it became the *genius loci* for that monument."

"I bet that's not in the tourist brochure," Richard said.

"But the fire spirit we saw didn't radiate heat except when it first manifested and when it attacked us," Lucas said.

"That's because it's associated with the sun," Richard explained. "It can be warm or burning, helpful or harmful. Our boy Harald was being clever. If he had summoned one of your typical fire spirits, he and his gang of butch young lovers might have burned to death instead of frozen."

Lucas studied the map. Maeshowe was labeled not only as a national park, but also as a UNESCO World Heritage Site.

"How did the practitioners get in to do the ritual?" he asked.

"They broke in, like we always do," Richard said.

"I don't think it's as easy to get into there as it is the little local monuments we've broken into."

"Probably not," Aunt Mary said. "Perhaps they have a contact within Parks Scotland."

"I wish we knew more about these people," Lucas said.

"Sadly, we don't, and we won't until you get up there," Aunt Mary said.

Lucas and Richard looked at each other.

"I'm already on vacation," his friend said.

"And I don't have any looming orders," Lucas said. "How do we get Della to come along?"

Richard grinned. "You need turn on the charm, darling."

Aunt Mary looked out the window at the bleak winter landscape and then turned to her nephew with a conspiratorial smile.

"I'll get Della to brew up some tea, and you fetch some of your uncle's Scotch. He'll want some when he gets back from the fields, and we might as well start without him."

Ten minutes later, they all sat in the living room sipping tea spiked with some very fine single malt scotch. Too fine to mix with tea, really, Lucas thought, but if they were going to convince Della to fly all the way up to Orkney, it was best to bring out the heavy artillery.

They sat chatting about what they had learned. Della had found nothing relevant in her studies while hidden away in the kitchen. That hardly came as a surprise. She had never even opened a book on the occult until a couple of months ago. She didn't know what to look for.

Nevertheless, she listened intently. Once she had heard everything, she turned to Richard.

"You didn't see or hear anything last night at Montague's house, did you?"

"Nothing at all. I even tried reaching the poor old chap, but it was a no go. I'm not sure what's happened with his spirit."

"I'll try and communicate with him," Aunt Mary said. "You have enough to do as it is."

"Thanks, Auntie," Richard said. "Did anyone else experience anything unusual last night?"

Lucas and Della both answered no, then Della

quickly added, "Oh, I had a weird thing happen last night. Sebastian called me."

Lucas's ears perked up. He had avoided asking her about that.

"Why is that so strange?" he asked in as casual a voice as he could muster. "I thought you two ended up friends."

Richard grinned at him. Lucas shot him a venomous look.

Della seemed not to notice. "We haven't really been friends since... well, you know. We've chatted a couple of times. He wanted to meet, so we went for a pint. He's worried about all this occult stuff."

Richard leaned forward. "So he's believing in it now?"

"I wouldn't say that. He's confused, just like I was. Just like I *am*. He admitted that the beings that attacked me in my apartment didn't look quite human."

"Did he admit he had some power over them?" Richard asked. "That boy has got some of the Talent. I could feel it."

"When?" Della asked.

"I tried to approach him a couple of times at The Knight Errant. He gave me the brush off."

"He probably thought you were trying to pull

him," Lucas said, enjoying the awkward expression this produced in Della.

"Oh, honey, no. Shivering newbies are not my style at all. His power was the only thing I was trying to feel. Strange that he would get in touch right when we're facing trouble."

"Synchronicity?" Lucas asked.

"Well, it wasn't coincidence because that doesn't exist," Aunt Mary said.

"He said he wants to help me. He seemed worried," Della said.

"Encourage him," Richard said. "I'm curious to see what forces moved him in your direction at a moment like this. If he's got as much Talent as I think he does, he could be of use to us. If only I could get him to relax enough to have a chat. I'm curious about him, and no, Lucas, not that way. Get your mind out of the gutter."

"Whatever you might have planned will have to wait for another day," Aunt Mary said. "You need to get up to Orkney and get to the bottom of this."

"I have ten more days left of my vacation," Richard said. "Lucas, you said you don't have any pressing orders?"

"I just shipped an end table the other day. My next project isn't due for a month."

"Good," Richard said. "Della, you'll have to speak with your professors."

"Wait, I can't just go flying off to Orkney. I have lectures to attend!"

"Call in sick."

"But I'm not sick, and I'm not going to lie to my professors."

"Call in bored."

"Bored?"

"Bored of your mundane life. Surely going to the farthest reaches of Scotland hunting spirits with us is preferable to sitting in a lecture hall or library all day, isn't it?"

"No."

Richard raised his face and hands toward the sky.

"Hopeless! Utterly hopeless! Lucas, speak with her."

"We need you," Lucas said.

"Oh, all right."

Richard blinked. "Is that all it took? Being cute and straight?"

"Stop," Lucas and Della said at the same time. Aunt Mary put on a poker face.

"We'll need to buy open-ended tickets," Richard said, unfazed. "I'll look into them. Lucas, could you check out hotels? No, perhaps an Airbnb would be better. More privacy. At this time of year, there must be no shortage of availability. Has anyone here been to Orkney?"

No one replied.

Wonderful, Lucas thought. *We're going to a place none of us is familiar with in order to face a danger we can't name and don't know how to stop.*

And this time it's not just our own lives at stake, it's the whole human race.

8

IT TURNED out that they couldn't get a flight for another three days. There were no direct flights from London to Kirkwall, the small town that passed for the capital of the Orkney Islands. They had to fly through Aberdeen then get a connecting flight to Kirkwall that only ran twice a week in the winter.

At least finding an Airbnb proved easy enough. From what Della read on the internet, Orkney enjoyed a brief period of tourism at the height of summer. At other times of the year, with long nights, cloudy and cold days, and nearly constant rain, the only people visiting were people who absolutely had to.

That, unfortunately, included them.

At least she got a breather from normal life. She went to lectures, read in the library, and tried to pretend everything was all right.

That worked for all of a day before Sebastian called again. He wanted to meet for lunch at an inexpensive dumpling place on Little Clarendon Street. The cheerful Chinese owners, a husband and wife team, always had a friendly greeting for everyone. Della wondered how people could have such sunny dispositions in a world filled with evil. Ignorance was bliss.

Della couldn't figure out a way to say no, so she said yes.

It helped that Sebastian was offering to pay. The flights to Orkney weren't cheap, even at this time of year.

"I've been thinking about what you said," Sebastian told her after they had sat down with their food. It was the lunch rush, and the buzz of conversation around them ensured their privacy. "I think perhaps there is something more to this than I see."

Della stared at him in surprise. That was sudden. She thought she had scared him off with that conversation at The Eagle and Child. Apparently he really had been giving it some thought.

Wait. He's not trying to get back together with me, is he?

No, you idiot. You don't even want that.

Right?

"There's a lot more to this than meets the eye," Della said. "I could give you some books to read, if you like. Not everything in them is true. Much of it is nonsense or pretty far from reality, but there are a lot of people, including some really bad people, who believe every word."

Aunt Mary had lent her some introductory books to ease her into this new world and had said the very same things to her.

Of course, it turned out that most everything in those books was completely true. A little white lie. Della could forgive the kindly old woman for sparing her sanity, at least in the short term.

"I have enough of a reading list this term," Sebastian said. "I'm more interested in the kind of people who do these things. That day you caught... that day you saw me at The Knight Errant, you were speaking with Richard Camilo. Do you see him often?"

"He's become a friend."

"Maybe, um, maybe I should speak with him. He approached me about it once or twice, and I gave him the cold shoulder. He sounds knowledgeable, though."

Another surprise. Even more, Sebastian looked guilty as hell for suggesting it. Was he interested in more than just occult knowledge?

Della couldn't figure out what she thought about that. Jealous? Not quite. Outraged? If he was trying to get his ex-girlfriend to hook him up with a man, she would have every right to be. Suspicious?

Yes, a bit suspicious, although she couldn't put her finger on why.

You're getting paranoid, she told herself. *This is just a good man, a confused but good man, stumbling toward the truth.*

And you've been doing plenty of your own stumbling lately, so don't judge.

"I could give him your number."

Sebastian made a face. "I wouldn't want him to misunderstand."

"I could explain it to him."

"Perhaps we could all meet together?"

"Sure, sometime. I'm going to be... going away for a bit."

Sebastian looked startled. "Going away?"

"For a few days. Maybe a week or two." *Or a month. Or a year. Or I might die.*

"Where?"

"To Orkney. You know, those islands to the north of Scotland?"

Sebastian nodded. "I know them well. I've been a couple of times. An old school chum lives up there. Why in the world are you going up there? Some new excavation? It hardly seems the time of year to do that."

Della blinked. He had been to Orkney? What were the chances? Richard and Lucas were always talking about synchronicities, strange intersections of events that pointed out hidden connections between people.

"How well do you know the place?" she asked.

Sebastian shrugged. "Well enough. The first time I spent a couple of weeks. The second time I spent a month. It's quite lovely in summer. Peaceful too. A good place for quiet study. You'd love the archaeology, and there are some incredible land-scapes and wildlife. But the winter is a wretched time to go."

She heard the question in his voice. She ate a dumpling and sipped her orange juice as an excuse not to answer at once.

"I'm going with Richard and... Lucas, another friend. I think I mentioned him."

"Oh. Is this some sort of paranormal investigation?"

Della studied him. There was no hint of a joke in his tone. In fact, there was a little tremor of fear. She sighed. "Yes. I don't know how long we'll be gone."

"Can you tell me about it?"

"I'm not sure I should." *You might think I'm absolutely crazy.*

"You can trust me." When Della gave him a look, he hastened to continue. "I mean, I'm not going to tell anyone or judge you. I know I'm on the Permanent Register of Despicable Boyfriends, but I worry about you. You've seemed terribly stressed ever since meeting these people."

"True enough," Della grumbled, spearing another dumpling.

"So tell me."

Oh God, he's giving me that puppy dog look with those big brown eyes of his.

Della caved, at least partly. "Oh, all right. It's another cult. Richard was friends with an occult bookdealer, the best in the country. The man... died. Richard was left with the responsibility of selling off the estate. Now every occultist in the United Kingdom is after the books. They're worth a fortune, and many of them are one of a kind. There seems to be a group up in Orkney who are behind it all."

"So why not call the police?"

"Because we have no proof." *Spotting a fire demon does not constitute proof in today's legal system. Funny how the Middle Ages was actually more advanced in some ways.*

"But you know they're behind it."

"Yes, from the way they operate. Certain types of magicians perform their rituals in certain ways. Some focus on different schools of magic while others use rituals particular to a specific region. The ones we're seeking are performing rituals only known in the Orkney Islands. So we know it's them. We need to go to Orkney to gather evidence against them."

Sebastian snapped his fingers. "Bjorn might be of help."

"Who's Bjorn?"

"The friend I mentioned. He's a graduate student at the Institute for Northern Studies there. He studies the folklore of the Orkney and Shetland Islands."

Della leaned back, stunned. "He sounds perfect."

"He's perfect in many ways. I think you'd like him."

"What is that supposed to mean?"

"He's a keen student, just like you, and while he specializes in folklore, he has an interest in archaeology. Quite the looker as well. And straight. That's certainly an advantage."

Della's brow furrowed. "Are you trying to set me up with your friend?"

Sebastian spread out his hands and gave that ironic smile she used to like so much.

"I will never be done apologizing to you. Perhaps this will go a little way toward me being forgiven."

"I'm not looking to hook up at the moment, thank you very much. But give me his number. He could be useful."

"I can introduce you in person."

"He's here in Oxford?"

"No. I mean I want to come up with you."

"What?"

"You're going into danger. I can't let you face it alone."

"I won't be facing it alone. I'll have Richard and Lucas there."

"I mean I can't let you face it without someone rational by your side."

"They're rational!" *Sort of.*

Sebastian made a calming gesture. "Maybe so. They sound like they're too far into this to see clearly, though. At least that's the impression Richard gives."

"You barely know him."

"Please let me do this, Della. I could never forgive myself if I sat by and you got hurt. If these Orcadian chaps are anything like Dr. Olding's friends, you are going into serious danger."

"What about your coursework?"

"What about yours? This sounds more important. I mean, your safety. I'll reserve judgment on wizards and fairies and leprechauns. I can be of help. I know the area and I'm good friends with Bjorn. Think about it." Sebastian checked his watch. "Now if you'll excuse me, I have a lecture to attend. If I'm going to be skipping a week's worth of them, I'd best go to all the ones I can. Please think about this."

"I will."

As soon as Sebastian left, Della called Richard and told him all about the conversation.

"This is perfect! He *must* come. Can't you see the connections building up one on top of the other? He called you just at the right time. He wants to speak with me. He even has a contact in the remote part of Scotland we need to go to!"

"Where will he stay?" Della sure didn't want to share a room with him.

"Oh, another synchronicity. I just rented an Airbnb in downtown Kirkwall, near the Folklore Society, and it just so happens to have five bedrooms. I got it dead cheap because of the time of year. The lady I spoke with only had a three bedroom and a five bedroom, and since I didn't want you and Lucas to keep me up all night with your loud lovemaking, I got the five bedroom."

"Wait. Why wouldn't the three-bedroom place have been enough for us?"

"Because Cassandra is coming."

Della groaned. Richard did not help matters by cackling.

"I'm not sure this is a good idea," Della said.

"Cassandra is an accomplished mage, and she specializes in water magic. That might be helpful on an island."

"I meant bringing Sebastian with us."

"He has the Talent, darling. I'd bet a thousand pounds on it. And what are the chances that, when the whole Dr. Olding affair blew up, Lucas and I would find not one but two people with an affinity for magic?"

"He doesn't know what he's getting into, and once he's in it, he won't want to be there, and he won't be able to get out," Della said, speaking from bitter experience.

"He already volunteered," Richard said softly. "He's an adult, and he can make his own decisions. His experience with Old Mother Shipton and Wayland the Smith was enough to give him a hint of what he's up against. And this is also part of his awakening to his real self. Magical ability cannot stay dormant forever, and it often comes out at the same time an individual makes another major life change."

Della thought about how her own magical ability began to manifest shortly after moving to a new country and getting serious with her career as an archaeologist.

"Is that what happened with you?" she asked.

"You mean did I leap out of the closet, sequins and tiaras flashing, at the same time I started shooting spells left and right? As a matter of fact, I did. It was a break from my old self, the one society tried to constrain me to. That's what your dear little boy is doing now. He's halfway there."

"I guess I can tell him he can come," Della grumbled.

"Your utter lack of enthusiasm fairly drips from every word."

"I have a bad feeling about this."

"He stomped on your heart in a most public and humiliating way. You have every right to steer clear of the chap. But he needs us. More importantly, I have a feeling we need *him*. Don't let your emotions cloud your judgment. We're up against some pretty dark forces, my friend."

Della smiled, her heart warming. She had never had very many friends, and those simple words always meant so much to her. Silly that she would be in such a fragile emotional state at her age. She should have gotten over that in her angsty teens. Sadly, she had grown into her angsty twenties with all her insecurities intact.

Come on, she told herself. *You've faced cults, ghosts, and fire demons. You've even been in a sword-fight. When are you going to start feeling good about yourself?*

If it were only that simple.

Perhaps confidence comes from force of habit.

"All right, I'll invite my cheating ex-boyfriend along with us," Della said.

"Good girl."

Sebastian did not prove popular with the rest of the group. When they met at the airport for their flight to Aberdeen, Cassandra immediately tried to hit on him. Sebastian showed no interest and didn't tell her why. Shocked at being ignored by a man she assumed to be straight, she fell into a sulk for the rest of the day. That was fine by Della.

Lucas also didn't take a shine to him. Della didn't see any real point of tension—the two simply did not exchange anything more than the common courtesies. But to do that for the length of an all-day trip spoke volumes.

On the other hand, Sebastian and Richard talked almost incessantly. They sat side by side on the flight. At first Sebastian tried to draw Richard out on occultism, but the older man told him he'd rather not speak of it in public, and Sebastian dropped the matter. Instead, Richard asked him to tell them about Orkney.

"Fascinating place," Sebastian said. "A bit small, and the nightlife is all but nonexistent, but if you like country walks, nature, and archaeology, you'll find it fascinating."

"This isn't exactly a sightseeing trip."

"No. I'd like to learn more about what sort of trip this is exactly."

"Later. Tell us more about Orkney."

"Hmm, where shall I start? It's easy enough to hire a car, so that won't be a problem. And we'll need one. The bus system is quite limited, although the ferries are good. There are also flights from island to island. With the winter winds coming along, I'd rather do the ferries, though."

"I heard on some quiz show they have the shortest flight in the world," Richard said.

"Yes, they're quite proud of it. It's between Westray and Papa Westray. There's less than three kilometers between them, and the flight only takes a minute. Literally a minute. The chap who used to fly it has the record for the most takeoffs and landings of any commercial pilot."

"You're quite the font of information," Richard said.

"Sebastian wins all the pub quizzes," Della said.

"I can imagine. Sadly, we probably won't be going on that flight. I think we'll mostly be on the Mainland," Richard said.

"Just Mainland," Sebastian said. "That refers to the biggest island. If you say 'the mainland,' they'll think you're referring to Scotland proper."

Lucas groaned, rolled his eyes, and returned to the book he was reading.

Sebastian didn't seem to notice, or he chose not to notice. "There are about seventy islands in total."

"Aha!" Richard said, elbowing him. "Something you don't know. How can you win pub quizzes if you don't know the precise number of islands in an obscure northern archipelago?"

"Aha to you," Sebastian said, elbowing him back. "I say 'about' because it depends on your definition of an island. Some are skerries."

"What's a skerry?" Della asked.

"A rock sticking out of the sea."

"Aren't all islands just rocks sticking out of the sea?"

"Yes, they are, and hence the problem. So what's an island and what's a skerry? Ask three Orcadians in a pub that question and you'll get five answers. Believe me, I tried it once. Quite amusing. The traditional definition is that a skerry is unfit for human habitation, but in that case one would have to call most council estates skerries. Besides, there's a skerry in Kirkwall harbor that was used as a prison in Viking times. They'd leave men stranded on there, and passing ships would toss them food. So it was a skerry but had a permanent, if small, population."

"The Vikings were such charmers," Richard said. "So, tell me about this Bjorn fellow. He sounds like a Viking."

"More of a mild-mannered Danish graduate student. He's on loan from the University of Aarhus to work on his dissertation on the folklore of the northern islands. He's been all over the North Atlantic—Orkney, the Shetland Islands, even the Faroes. You'd like him. He specializes in the folklore related to ancient sites."

Richard caught Della's eye. The occultist was always talking about synchronicities. This was a big one.

"Yes," Richard murmured. "I think I'd like to speak with him about that."

They had a layover in Aberdeen airport, where they ate an overpriced and unsatisfying lunch then boarded a small propeller-driven plane for the final leg of their journey. The plane didn't look like it could hold more than fifty people, and it was only about half-full. Della had never been on a plane so small. Rain drummed on the wings as they taxied down the runway.

As luck would have it, she got stuck next to Cassandra, who was clutching the armrest in a white-knuckle grip and staring straight ahead.

Della had the window seat and glanced out. The airport had faded into an indistinct smudge. The runway was awash with rain.

The motor revved as they picked up speed. A strong wind buffeted the plane, shaking it back and forth as it headed for takeoff.

Cassandra turned pale and gripped the armrest tighter.

"You all right?" Della asked.

"I hate flying in rough weather," Cassandra said through clenched teeth. "It's beastly out."

"We'll be all right," Della said, as much to reassure herself as her travel companion. She wasn't a nervous flier, but with weather like this, she hardly felt relaxed either.

The plane rose into the air, bucked, lost altitude —eliciting a hiss from Cassandra— then steadied out and began to climb.

The runway, the airport, and the earth itself disappeared into a gray soup. The plane lurched to the side as it got slammed by a crosswind and lost a bit of altitude then continued to rise. A moment later, it was hit by a series of quick jerks as if it was a car with bad shock absorbers going over a series of potholes.

Cassandra was beginning to turn green, actually

green. Della watched her with fascination. She had always thought that was a figure of speech.

"How are you doing?" Della asked.

"Urg."

That wasn't exactly the most eloquent statement she had ever heard pass Cassandra's lips, but Della felt sure it neatly summarized the mage's feelings at the moment.

The airplane dropped again, sending their stomachs to the ceiling, before leveling out.

"Unnngh."

Cassandra doubled over, clutching at her mouth.

Della grabbed an air-sickness bag, opened it, and shoved it into the woman's hands.

Just in time. Cassandra retched, coughed, then spewed into the bag.

Serves you right for flirting with my ex-boyfriend, Della thought.

A second later, the cabin filled with the terrible stench of Cassandra's half-digested airport lunch.

Now it was Della's turn to feel sick. She held her hand over her nose, trying and failing to keep out the smell. She searched for her air-sickness bag in the seat pocket in front of her, only to remember that she had given it to Cassandra. The woman was still hunched over, losing the last bits of her lunch, so

Della couldn't reach into Cassandra's seat pocket and get her bag.

The plane bucked and danced, tossed about by the wind and hammered by the driving rain. There was nothing to see out the window. Della hoped they had gained some altitude. Weren't there tall mountains in northern Scotland? What if they slammed into one? A little plane like this still had radar, right?

A stewardess came along the aisle, walking with a bowlegged gait and holding onto the seats to either side. She stopped and leaned over Cassandra.

"Are you all right, ma'am?" she asked in a matronly Scottish accent.

Blurp. Another bit of lunch dropped into the bag.

To her credit, the stewardess didn't bat an eyelid.

"I'll just take this," she said, gingerly relieving Cassandra of her now-full air-sickness bag. Cassandra immediately grabbed the spare one and opened it.

"Excuse me," Della said. "I could use—"

But the stewardess was already gone.

If I have to throw up, I'll throw up on Cassandra. She deserves it.

For another hour, the plane bucked and dove. Cassandra filled up another bag, the stench nauseating Della. Somehow, she managed not to spoil Cassandra's dress. That was a disappointment. It would have made Della feel better.

Gradually the weather eased, and the plane got onto a steady course. The pilot came on the intercom and in an annoyingly cheery voice welcomed them to Scottish weather and announced it was clearing up ahead.

Della peered through the window. It looked the same uniform dark gray that it had been for the entire trip. At least the air circulation system had taken away the worst of the smell. Della's stomach stopped threatening to avenge itself on Cassandra.

The plane started to descend. She cast a nervous glance at her travel companion. She looked drawn, but better.

The clouds began to brighten, suddenly opening up to a breathtaking view.

The plane had descended lower than Della had suspected, scudding over a brilliant blue sea crested with the white foam of choppy waves. Behind them, a rough landmass and sheer cliffs dwindled in the distance. The last of the Scottish mainland.

Up ahead came the first of the islands—a pair of small rocks jutting out of the sea, waves crashing over them.

Skerries, Della corrected herself with a smile. *With Sebastian along, I have to be precise about everything.*

Next came a proper island, a cliff-bound oval of green that didn't look more than a couple of kilometers long. There wasn't a single tree on it, but remarkably, she spotted a pair of cottages and a scattering of white dots she presumed to be a flock of sheep.

The plane descended farther, passing over the tiny island and coming to some more skerries, some jutting like stone fingers out of the sea, others barely humping above the surface and looking like the backs of motionless whales. The sunlight was out now, sparking off the blue water. They approached another island, a larger one this time, where waves crashed and foamed against a jagged shoreline of stones carved into weird shapes by the wind and surf.

This island took longer to fly over, its undulating green fields spreading out like a carpet below them. Still they descended, and a few little clusters of cottages stood out clearly beneath them. Della spotted cultivated fields and large flocks of sheep and cows.

Then they were past that island and once again over the glittering water, a blue sheen flecked with white and studded with skerries for a brief stretch before they came over another island. Green fields stretched as far as the little window allowed her to see.

"This is Mainland," Sebastian said from the other aisle. "We're almost there."

The ground drew closer, a lush field of green. In the distance, Della spotted a town, the first she had seen since takeoff. Then the tarmac rushed up at them, and they touched down. Della felt sorry the wonderful sights were over.

Within a minute, the rain had started up again. A black wall of clouds swept over the airport and dropped a torrent of rain on the plane as it taxied to the terminal.

"I hope it's not like this the entire time," Cassandra said. She looked relieved to be back on the ground.

"I checked the weather for this week," Richard said.

Cassandra turned to him. "And?"

"You don't want to know."

They took a pair of taxis from the airport to Kirkwall, shooting along a narrow highway buffeted with wind. Della shared a taxi with Richard and Sebastian. Cassandra and Lucas took the other, and Della wondered if the woman, having failed with Sebastian, was back to her old tricks.

The beautiful view from the plane had been all too brief. Now, as the rain flowed down the window in a continuous sheet, she could only see a vague outline of fields and the occasional building. Whenever a vehicle passed in the opposite direction, a wave of water thudded against the glass.

Sebastian pulled out his phone. "I told Bjorn we were coming. I'll just ring him up and see if he can meet us."

As he got on the phone and made small talk with his friend, Richard turned to Della.

"How are you feeling?"

"Relieved not to be sitting next to a puking society girl."

"That stank badly enough on our side of the aisle. I can't imagine what it was like for you." He lowered his voice. "But I meant, are you feeling anything unusual?"

"I'm not as sensitive as you think I am."

"Incorrect. You're more sensitive than you think you are."

Della sighed. On the last case, they had made her pass a hand over a map, looking for disrupted points on the ley lines. Oddly, that had actually worked. Right now, though, she didn't feel a thing.

"You're distracted by the flight," Richard said, then made a little nod to Sebastian, who chattered away, oblivious. "And by some of the company you're keeping."

"I really don't need all this drama," Della whispered.

"Sor-ry," Richard said in a singsong voice. "How about you clear your mind and focus for a bit?"

Della did as he asked and got sucked into another world almost immediately.

9

"DELLA FELT SOMETHING," Richard told Lucas as they struggled through the rain from the taxi to their front door at the apartment complex in Kirkwall where they had rented an Airbnb. It couldn't have been more than twenty meters, but they still managed to get soaked.

They stopped inside the front door as Cassandra and the estate agent went up the stairs. Sebastian and Della followed, struggling with their bags. Cassandra had left hers on the landing for someone else to carry. That didn't surprise Lucas. She had grown up with servants.

After the others had gotten to the upstairs landing and everyone was chattering away, Lucas asked in a low voice, "What did she sense? I felt some ripples in the ley lines we passed, but Cassandra kept distracting me by putting her hand on my lap."

Richard laughed. "Did you see her face when our little Sebastian cold-shouldered her? Priceless."

"Priceless indeed, but now she's not focusing on the job. There's something up with the ley lines here, and she was mucking about so much she didn't feel it. What did Della feel?"

"Not your lap, that's for sure."

"Please be serious for once."

Richard smiled then replied in a level tone, "She felt the same pulsation in the ley lines you and I did, and a sort of sour taste to her mouth. I asked her to close her eyes, and after a minute, they snapped right open and her face went all pale. Sebastian was still gabbling away with his Danish friend on the phone and didn't notice."

"Did she see something?"

"Faces in the darkness, glowering at her. She said they were hideously ugly, unnaturally wide with dirty skin and bulging eyes."

"Like trolls?"

"The popular depiction of them, at least."

"Did she see Montague?"

"No."

"Did she try again?"

"I didn't have the heart to ask her. It put her well out of sorts."

Lucas had reached out to the dead bookseller several times since he had seen him during the ritual, but while he had felt the faint glimmerings of contact, he had never heard his voice or seen his face.

He paused for a moment, letting his mind go blank and opening his senses as Aunt Mary had taught him to.

"I'm not feeling anything now."

"Neither am I. There are no ley lines through this town. No shortage in the countryside, though. I've always heard this place is one of the great ley centers of Europe."

"Yes, those maps certainly say so." He had brought Aunt Mary's maps with him. "So, what's with Sebastian? He was talking your ear off through both flights."

Richard shrugged. "It's odd. I don't think he's trying to pull me, but his attitude has changed completely. He always avoided me at The Knight Errant, and now he clings to me like a limpet."

"I heard him ask you about the magical arts, and you shut him down."

"I'm not going to chat about that sort of thing on

an airplane. I get profiled enough while flying, thank you very much. But that's the strangest thing of all. Back in Oxford, every time I tried to talk to him about it, he ran off."

"What changed?"

"No idea. One thing I do know is that he's definitely got the Talent. I could feel it on him." Richard poked Lucas in the belly. "Don't make the obvious joke."

Cassandra popped her head out the door and called down the stairs to them.

"Are you two coming?"

"All right," Lucas said.

"Oh, be a darling and bring up my bag. I forgot it on the landing."

Shaking his head, Lucas grabbed her bag as well as his own.

They went up and unpacked. The flat was roomy and soulless, with IKEA furniture and minimal decoration, and obviously never used by the woman who actually owned it. Cassandra complained that they were slumming. Through his bedroom window, all Lucas could see was a narrow, rainy street of tidy little houses painted bright blues and yellows that tried and failed to look cheery in the gloom. He felt a long way from home and suddenly very lonely. A stupid thing to feel, he told himself. He had a flat full of friends here.

Well, no, that wasn't true. He had Richard. Cassandra was an annoyance, Sebastian an irritating stranger, and Della... well, he didn't know what Della was.

By the time he had unpacked and changed into something dry, late afternoon sunlight was streaming through the window. Peering out, he saw patches of blue through the clouds. Now those houses across the street really did look cheery, at least for the moment. He went out to the common room to find Richard and Sebastian chatting on the sofa and Della and Cassandra sitting side by side, each pretending the other didn't exist. Cassandra was texting, and Della was staring out at the rain with a stricken look.

Rain? In the time it had taken to pass from one room to the other, the weather had turned again. Lucas had a feeling it did that a lot up here.

I need to talk to her about what she saw, Lucas thought, *but not in this crowd. Cassandra will no doubt say something catty, and Sebastian wouldn't believe a word of it.*

Richard motioned for Lucas to join him in his room. He led him to the closet, where he opened the sliding door to show a heavy parcel wrapped in black paper. Around it was a circle of red powder. Several glyphs were written in the same powder around it.

"The books?" Lucas guessed.

"Yes."

"Don't you think it's a risk bringing them up here?"

"Not as much of a risk as leaving them unguarded in London or Oxford. There are warding sigils on the paper they're wrapped in. Plus, they're inside a circle made from protective powder."

"Won't they sense that the books have been moved?"

"Not with the spells I put on that wrapping. They're as safe as they can be."

Lucas smiled. "We better hope the cleaning lady doesn't spot it."

"No cleaning lady for a week, according to the contract. If we're not done by then, I have a feeling we'll be too late."

"I don't think I could stand more than a week of Sebastian's nonstop lecturing."

Richard pinched his cheek. "You're just jealous because he's cuter than you. Let's go join the others."

When they returned to the living room, Sebastian looked up from his phone.

"We're going to meet with Bjorn at The Reel in

fifteen minutes. It's a nice pub not far from here. Actually, everything in Kirkwall isn't far from here. It's a bit early for a pint, but he's a Dane so he won't mind."

Lucas glanced at the window, which was almost pitch-black now. "Doesn't look early to me."

"It's not even five. You're in the north now."

By the time they got to The Reel, a snug little pub next to the Romanesque cathedral of red sandstone in central Kirkwall, it was dark. Lucas got the impression that even if the skies had been clear, it wouldn't make any difference. He wondered if so much night here in the winter affected the local magic.

The pub's interior was a single large room with a stage to one side. Bright lighting made it feel more like a café. Generally, Lucas preferred more subdued lighting in a pub, but considering the weather, he understood why they had lit the place up. Sebastian called out to a husky man in his middle twenties with a blond buzz cut sitting at a big table in the corner. The two embraced. After introductions, they all got a pint and sat down.

"Sebastian tells me you're up here for a uni project," Bjorn said in good English with only the lightest of accents. Lucas had always been impressed with how well Scandinavians learned English. Although, on second thought, that wasn't so surprising. It wasn't like Danish was much use outside of Denmark.

"That's right," Lucas said, going along with the cover story they had previously arranged. "Della and I are both studying folklore as it relates to archaeological sites. Richard and Casandra are folklorists as well."

"We do have real jobs, though," Cassandra said.

Lucas tried to kick her but only managed to stub his toe on the table leg. Why did she have to act superior all the time? They needed this fellow, and from the flicker of irritation that passed over his pale features, Cassandra's snobbery wasn't helping make him a useful contact.

Luckily, the Dane chose to ignore the remark and replied, "That's wonderful. You'll find plenty of useful material up here on the islands."

Sebastian smiled. "And I'm just along for the ride. I needed to get away from my thesis for a bit."

"And you chose to come to Orkney in winter! You always were a bit daft, Sebastian." Bjorn turned to Della. "You've come to the right place. The islands resonate with folklore, and although so much has been lost in more populated parts of the country, it's still very much alive here. All the islanders are proud of their past and learn the old stories from their grandparents."

"We'd like to see some of the archaeological sites in person," Lucas said.

"I'll show you them myself," Bjorn said, not taking his eyes off Della. "The first place you should see is the Ring of Brodgar. I'm sure you've seen pictures. One of the most impressive stone circles anywhere. Then there's Maeshowe, it's a—"

"A Neolithic cairn," Della said. "Yes, I've read all about it. Fascinating. I'm looking forward to seeing the runes."

"It's an impressive place. Sebastian told me you've excavated Neolithic sites down south, so I know you'll love this. I'm sure you've heard all about the Norse runes left there during a snowstorm, but here's a little bit of local lore that's less well-known. We not only know about the Norsemen sheltering in Maeshowe from the runes they left, but also from the *Orkneyinga Saga*, a Norse saga about events in Orkney assembled in the early thirteenth century. It's great fun to read, a mix of history and legend. Because of the legend part, much of the history hasn't been taken seriously. For example, we already knew about the Norse hiding in Maeshowe before we excavated it."

"It's mentioned in the saga?" Cassandra asked, leaning forward and putting a hand on his arm.

He glanced at her, said, "Yes, it is," and turned back to Della.

Cassandra withdrew her hand.

"How does the passage go? Ah, yes." The Dane closed his eyes. "'On the thirteenth day of Christmas, they traveled on foot over to Firth. During a snow-storm, they took shelter in Maeshowe and two of them—' that's his men '—went insane, which slowed them down badly so that by the time they reached Firth, it was nighttime.' Now, we've always had this saga, but it wasn't until Maeshowe was excavated in 1861 that we actually found proof in the form of the runes."

"You know your onions," Lucas said.

Bjorn looked at him curiously. "What?"

Lucas cleared his throat, flustered. "English expression. You know what you're talking about. Go on."

Della laughed. "The English have an endless supply of silly sayings."

Bjorn laughed along with her. "They do!"

Lucas seethed as the conversation went on without him.

"So, tell me more about Maeshowe?" Della asked, leaning forward. Did she actually bat her eyes at this fellow? No, he must be mistaken.

"Oh, you'll love this. The runic graffiti includes a passage in which the Norsemen said that before they broke in, another group had broken in some years before them and had taken a great treasure away to somewhere to the northwest. In 1858, a Viking silver horde weighing sixteen pounds was found near the Bay of Skaill, seven miles to the northwest of Maeshowe."

"Wow, so Norse folklore got confirmed by archaeology!" Della said.

"Incredible, isn't it?"

Della and Bjorn nattered on, completely ignoring the rest of the table. Cassandra tried to intervene several times, got brushed off, and lapsed into a sulk.

Lucas kept quiet too. At least Della was gathering a lot of good information.

Richard and Sebastian were chattering away a mile a minute as well, but about less useful things. Mostly they were talking about nightlife in Oxford and London. Once, the younger man tried to steer the conversation onto occultism, but Richard silenced him with a subtle shake of his head and suggested another round. Lucas went too.

The second round turned into a third, as it often did with Richard at the table. Sebastian seemed eager too. Lucas went along for the ride. He felt like a bit of a boozer tonight.

When the three men went back to the bar for the third time, Sebastian asked, "Do you think she's trying to make me feel jealous?"

"Who?" Lucas asked.

Richard elbowed him in the ribs. "He means Della, dummy, with Bjorn the Viking. No, Sebastian, it's not you she's trying to make jealous."

"I hope not," Sebastian said. "I've moved on. She needs to as well."

She has, you idiot, Lucas thought.

"Good beer," Lucas said, sipping his pint of dark, rich ale.

"Dark Island." Sebastian held his own pint high. "Brewed right here in Orkney. They distill some fine whiskey as well."

Richard perked up. "Whiskey?"

"It's not even seven, and we have work to do," Lucas said. If they got started on whiskey, they'd never get anything done.

"Looks like Della is doing all of it," Sebastian said. "Is this helping? Are you getting the information you want?"

"He's a useful contact. But there's a lot he won't know," Richard told him.

"But it's a start, right?"

"Yes, Sebastian."

He's sure eager, Lucas thought. *A bit too eager. Montague got himself killed by being too eager.*

When they returned, Bjorn was talking about local fairy legends.

"Fairies, my favorite!" Richard said.

Sebastian laughed, a little too loudly. It was only then that Lucas realized the three of them were already drunk. They hadn't eaten since an early lunch, and the local ale was stronger than most.

"Lots of fairies up here," Bjorn was saying, getting the joke and smiling to show he had no problem with it. "Elves too."

"I've always had a soft spot for elves," Della admitted.

"Really?" the Dane asked.

"I inhaled fantasy novels as a kid, especially Tolkien and the Forgotten Realms."

Sebastian smiled. "She used to call herself Lady Legolas."

Everyone burst out laughing.

Everyone, that is, except Della.

"Shut up!" she snapped.

They kept laughing.

"I was twelve. Shut up."

"Oh, honey," Richard said, wiping his eyes, "that is altogether too much. But you won't be laughing if we come across one. These aren't your metrosexual elves of the fantasy novels. These are the grim, dangerous, folkloric kind. The real kind."

"You believe there are real elves? Are you serious?" Bjorn asked. "I think you should stop laughing at Della now."

"Oh, they're serious," Della said, shaking her head. "And sad to say, they're probably right."

A silence settled over the table as everyone realized Richard had said too much. Bjorn looked around curiously and was about to say something when Lucas cut in.

"In folkloric studies we get a lot of silly stories, don't we, Della?"

"Oh, sure," she said quickly, eager to cover up their mistake.

Lucas decided the best way to cover it up was to defuse it.

"Down in London we have a haunting in every

street. I should take you to Pond Square and intro-duce you to the ghost chicken," he said.

Della rolled her eyes. "Here we go."

Bjorn laughed and nudged her as if they'd been friends for years.

Lucas smiled, both annoyed by the gesture and relieved that the tension had passed.

"What, don't you believe in the ghost chicken?" he asked in mock seriousness.

"No."

"If humans can manifest themselves as ghosts, why can't chickens?"

"Who says humans can?" Now Della was getting in on the act. She knew full well that ghosts existed.

"There's proof," Lucas said. He had decided to play the fool in order to ease the pressure.

Hey, at least he was back in the conversation.

"There are blurry photos and self-contradicting stories from confused witnesses," Della said.

Lucas raised a finger. "Ah, but the ghost chicken has a long and storied past and is associated with the great natural philosopher Sir Francis Bacon."

"Here we go." Della sighed.

Lucas went on, unperturbed.

"It was back in the bitterly cold winter of 1626 when Sir Francis Bacon decided to test one of his pet theories. You see, he had seen rats frozen in the streets of London, the city being even dirtier back then than now, and he had noted that they didn't decompose. He was visiting a friend who lived at Pond Square and discussed whether or not putting meat on ice might help preserve it. There weren't any refrigerators in those days, and the only way to preserve meat was to salt it like crazy, making the meat rather tough and unpalatable, even worse than those sandwiches we had at Aberdeen airport. So he bought a chicken, slaughtered and plucked it, and stuffed it with snow."

"A decent application of the scientific method," Della conceded.

"Yes, but it didn't work out so well for dear old Francis. He caught a chill that grew into a serious illness that took his life. Now, on dark nights, you can sometimes see the faint image of a headless chicken running through Pond Square."

Della and Bjorn laughed, both at the ridiculous story and at the fact that Lucas seemed to half believe it.

Lucas sat up straight, pretending to be offended. "You may mock, but it isn't funny for the many people who have seen it. It was most traumatic for them."

"My heart bleeds," Della said.

"We don't have ghost chickens here," Bjorn said, "but we have selkies, who are men who can turn themselves into seals. The northern islands have trolls, too, just like back in Denmark."

"We have those as well," Richard told Sebastian. "Dirty old men lurking in the shadows of clubs. Watch out for them."

Bjorn cocked his head. "You have something to tell me, Sebastian?"

"I came out of the closet recently," Sebastian said, blushing.

"Ha! We always knew. Your hair was too perfect," Bjorn said, eliciting a shriek of laughter from Richard.

Sebastian looked at him nervously. "So, you're all right with it?"

"Why wouldn't I be?" Bjorn gave him a playful punch on the shoulder. "Like I said, we've all known for years."

"Really?"

"Yes, really. Relax."

Della's brow furrowed. "Back to the subject at hand, tell us a bit about these trolls."

Oh, looks like we're going to talk about her vision after all. Good on you for bringing that up, Della,

Lucas thought, taking another pull from his pint. To his surprise, he discovered it to be half-empty already. He knew he shouldn't be drinking so much. With Cassandra and Sebastian along, though, how couldn't he? And this Bjorn fellow was irritating.

Sebastian looked abashed at his ex-girlfriend cutting him off.

Bjorn continued, utterly unaware of the drama he was creating. "Stories of trolls are found all over these islands, and the creatures tend to be a bit more threatening than the ones we have back home. You see, in Denmark, trolls aren't so bad if you give them proper respect. I come from the countryside, and in my grandmother's time, they used to leave a bowl of milk out every morning for the trolls. If you did that, they wouldn't hurt your cattle or steal your children. They might even help out with a bit of farmwork." Bjorn chuckled. "Silly to think that this was still believed in living memory. My grandmother was full of tales of trolls and fairies and witchcraft. That's where I got my interest in folklore."

"So how are the trolls here different?" Della asked, looking serious.

"Much more malign. They live in burial mounds or under the hills, and you have to propitiate them with offerings of food like my grandmother did. It didn't always work, though. They'd terrorize the household or make the livestock sick, and you'd have to call in a local cunning woman to make a charm to send them away."

"Do people still believe in them here?" Della asked.

Bjorn chuckled. "We're not that remote! Oh, there are still some old superstitions clinging to the older generation, but no one truly believes in trolls anymore. Or ghost chickens."

Bjorn gave Lucas a sly look. He didn't take the bait. Della didn't respond to the joke either. She seemed lost in thought.

After another round, Bjorn said he had things to do but would meet up with them the next day.

"I'm looking forward to showing you the sights," he told Della. "It's always nice to meet an archae-ologist."

They headed out. Thankfully, it wasn't raining at the moment. Richard had once again mixed busi-ness with pleasure, and Lucas's steps weren't too steady.

He still managed to fall in beside Della. "Sebast-ian's friend was a font of information."

Della's eyes lit up. "Yeah, he was amazing."

Suppressing his annoyance, Lucas said, "Richard told me you had a vision."

Della shuddered and glanced around the darkened streets. Most of the windows had curtains drawn, and there was little light. She looked over her shoulder to make sure Sebastian was busy talking to Richard and said quietly, "It was strange. All these ugly faces leering at me. They didn't look human. Their skin was this weird yellowish green, and they had these broad, flat faces and long noses. Big eyes too. Creepy eyes. Like trolls. That's why I asked him about them. You don't think they could be real, could they?"

Lucas sighed. "I've never thought they could be, but after having an acquaintance killed by ghosts and us getting attacked by a fire demon, I'm willing to believe in anything."

Della hung her head.

"Yeah, that's what I thought you'd say," she whispered.

10

DELLA HAD trouble sleeping that night. She never felt comfortable sleeping in strange places. She disliked hotels, and this Airbnb felt close enough to one.

She also had to admit that she felt nervous about dreaming. When Richard had asked her to close her eyes and focus while in the taxi on the way into town from the airport, she had been totally unprepared for how fast and strong the sensations came.

She'd felt the pulse of some strange power a few times as they drove, a power she had felt before and had been taught was that of the ley lines. Their power felt different this time. *Toxic* was the word that came into her head. And as the drive continued and her awareness of a problem with the ley lines grew, she felt a sudden jerk of power.

And then they were looking at her—a half-dozen strange faces peering at her with a mixture of curiosity and rage. There was no mistaking their hostility.

But what had they been? Could they really have been trolls, as Lucas had suggested?

Whatever they were, she did not want to close her eyes and see them again.

But she had to sleep. She and the rest of them were supposed to meet Bjorn and visit a couple of the major archaeological sites, including Maeshowe, where Aunt Mary said the fire spirit had probably originated.

Della knew there would be a heap of stress and trouble tomorrow.

At least she would get to sleep in, she thought with an ironic smile. This far north in October, the sun didn't even rise until seven thirty.

She planned on doing just that. The trip had been stressful. She'd been stuck all day with Cassandra, who she couldn't stand, plus Sebastian, who spent the entire time jabbering away with his new gay friend.

If you got to go off on a new lifestyle, fine, but do you have to shove my face in it?

Della sighed and turned in her bed.

And then the three of them got drunk while Cassandra went into a sulk because no one was paying attention to her. There had been a live concert of folk music that night, but Della hadn't felt like staying. She had been too tired. Bjorn said that The Reel had folk music several nights of the week and had invited her to join him for the next one.

She might just take him up on that. He was cute and funny and filled with fascinating knowledge. Most of all, he wasn't a wizard and didn't make a hobby of speaking with spirits. After all the weird turns her life had taken in recent months, that was a relief.

Too bad he lived way up here instead of in Oxford.

At last, sleep began to tug her down into its embrace. Snatches of visions from the dream world flashed through her mind. She awoke with a start and looked around the room. There was nothing to see.

Sleep pulled her down once again...

...and into a series of strange dreams.

First, she stood in a playground. A game of hopscotch was drawn in chalk on the pavement, along with a few childish drawings. A little girl with a crow's head was standing in the middle of a circle of other children who were all laughing and pointing at her. The girl clutched her head and let out a squawk. That only made the children laugh louder.

A matronly woman pushed through the crowd of children and slapped the crow girl on the face, turning her head back into a regular child's.

"That'll teach you not to forget what I've told you!" the woman shouted.

The scene shifted to a beach at night. Although the sky was overcast and there was no other light, Della could somehow see. A woman in a rough, homespun dress lay on the beach, weighed down by seven stones. She had one on each hand and foot, one on her forehead, and two on her chest.

"To thee! To thee!" she cried. "In your domain between the land and the sea!"

The scene shifted again, and she saw Montague atop a mound of grassy earth. Somehow she saw him both from a distance and from nearby, thus she could see the entire large mound on which he knelt and what he was doing in close-up detail. He knelt beside a small hole in the top of the mound, his tall, thin body folding up like a grasshopper's. He held a pint glass in his hand and poured the beer into the hole.

When he had poured half of it, he stopped and turned to Della.

"You have to give them some, but take care not to give them too much."

Della awoke with a start. Inside her room, it was pitch-black. To reassure herself, she turned on her phone, the light from the screen showing the simple guest room. Basic furniture. A photo of a puffin on the wall. Her suitcase sitting in a corner. Nothing else. She was about to try and go back to sleep when she heard movement and voices in the common area.

She checked her phone. To her surprise, it was just past seven in the morning.

"Time for a new day of weirdness," Della grumbled as she got dressed.

She did not go out immediately. First she sat at the end of her bed and tried to sort her thoughts. The strange series of short dreams remained fresh in her memory. They hadn't faded like regular dreams. And they had seemed far more real. The two that had taken place in the daytime had bright colors, unlike the muted colors typical of her dreams. And the one at night by the sea had been even more impressive. She had heard the surf, smelled the salt of the ocean, even felt the cold damp of the beach breeze.

She had no idea what either the dream about the

crow-headed girl or the one with the woman lying on the sand with the stones on her meant. The third one did ring a bell in her memory.

Some of the books she had read about Europe's prehistoric monuments talked about the folklore medieval and early modern people had attached to them. She had always skimmed those parts since they weren't scientifically relevant, but one tradition had been repeated often enough that it had stuck in her mind.

It had been common practice in the British Isles as well as Scandinavia to pour offerings through a hole dug in the top of burial mounds. These mounds were found all across Europe and were the burial places for people of local importance in the Neolithic and Bronze Age. For some burial mounds, knowledge of their original use had been somewhat retained in the form of wild legends about kings buried with fantastic treasure. This had the unfortunate effect of encouraging grave robbers who wrecked the archaeological context. A more common belief was that they were the homes of trolls or fairy folk. These creatures had to be propitiated, otherwise they could bring trouble on the local households. So it was common for the locals to pour offerings of beer, porridge, or other food into them. A silly superstition, but fear of the "wee folk" had kept many burial mounds from being destroyed.

So why was she dreaming about Montague doing that? What had he said? That you had to feed them but be careful not to feed them too much?

A few months ago, the old Della Marshal would have dismissed the dream as a random creation of her subconscious, a mingling of images taken from her reading colored by the shock and grief over losing an acquaintance.

Now she knew better. Now she knew that Montague had been trying to tell her something.

The question was—what?

She came out of her room to find Sebastian and Lucas slumped on the sofa looking a bit worse for wear and Richard in the kitchen cooking up breakfast. Cassandra was nowhere to be seen, thankfully.

"You're just in time for Richard's famous hangover special," Lucas said.

"I'm not hungover," she replied.

"Neither am I," Richard called over his shoulder. "Only these two amateurs. Wasn't that ale lovely? You should have tried the local whiskey. Simply scrumptious. We should go on adventures in the far north more often."

They sat down in the dining area to bacon,

tomato, and scrambled eggs washed down with black coffee.

"Cassandra was kind enough to do some shopping last night before barricading herself in her room," Richard said.

"Will she be joining us today?" Della asked.

"She has to," Richard said.

Sebastian took a long sip of his coffee and said, "Now that we're free to speak, can you fill me in a bit more about what this is all about?"

"Quite eager, aren't you?" Richard asked. "Well, as you know, there are people in this country who take occultism quite seriously, seriously enough to kill for it. We are searching for just such a group of people. A colleague of mine who was a dealer in rare occult books died, and I've been left to take care of his estate. While I was working through the books in his house in London, there were a couple of attempted break-ins. I was even attacked."

"Did you see who it was?"

"I didn't. He was wearing a mask. And I saw no point in informing the police because there was no evidence. I did find some clues through occult contacts that there was a demand for certain books my friend purchased from the estate of an occultist here in Orkney who passed away recently. I also found evidence that a group of Orcadian occultists are behind the break-ins and the attack on me."

Della marveled at how smoothly Richard told enough truth to fill Sebastian in but not so much as to make him think they were all completely bonkers.

I'm going to have to learn that skill, she mused.

"What sort of evidence?" Sebastian asked.

"There are certain rituals done only by certain local groups. The one done against me was done by an Orcadian occult circle. It might have been an individual, but more likely a group since it was so powerful."

Sebastian studied him for a moment. Della found his face, once so open and easy to read, inscrutable. How much did he believe, and what did he think of all of them?

Della found that she still cared what this foolish, confused man thought of her. Not that she wanted him back, but he had been a good friend once. She had never had many of those. It would be nice if he could be so again.

Sebastian looked at the three of them in turn and said, "So we're going to string my friend along, pumping him for information about local legends and not telling him he might be in danger?"

"He's not in any danger, at least not yet," Lucas

said. "It's the books they want. And we need to learn what Bjorn knows. The local occultists are basing their rituals, and their plan of attack, on local folk beliefs. If we're to stop them, we need Bjorn's help. At first I thought he'd just be a handy local guide, but his knowledge of these things is so deep I now see we need him a lot more than we first thought."

Sebastian frowned at him. "So, in other words, we're going to string him along and not tell him he's in danger."

"If we told him the truth, would he believe us?" Richard asked.

"No."

But do you believe? Della wondered. *What changed?*

Sebastian looked at his watch. "We're supposed to meet Bjorn at the Ring of Brodgar at nine."

"I'd like to get there a bit early," Richard said. "I hope the hangover cure is helping."

"I'm not an alcoholic," Sebastian said.

Richard blinked. "Nobody said you are, darling."

"You're not an alcoholic either, despite how much you drink," Sebastian told him then pointed to Lucas and Della. "And neither are you, or you."

"I'm not following," Della said.

"My uncle was an alcoholic," Sebastian said. "I

think I mentioned it once or twice, Della. I never gave you the full story because I never had much contact with him. I heard quite a lot from my family, though. His drinking wasn't bad at first, just the simple hefty weekend boozer that so many people do. Then it spread to weekdays. Then every day. The family raised their collective eyebrows but did nothing to intervene other than the occasional comment. Of course, he ignored them. Then it began affecting his work. He got skipped over for a promotion. Then he got caught drunk driving and lost his license. He needed the car for work, so he lost his job because of that. His children had to take out loans for uni, and his wife left him. He ended up on benefit and borrowing money from the rest of the family, money he couldn't, and wouldn't, ever pay back. He's still like that today. I never had to deal with any of that because my parents hardly ever let me see him, but in a way, I did because I never got to have an uncle in my life."

"I'm terribly sorry that happened to you," Lucas said. "But I fail to see how—"

Sebastian jabbed a finger at him, silencing him. Sebastian then looked at Richard and Della for a moment. "I'm beginning to think that occultism is a bit like drink. It can be a fun little diversion at first.

No one takes it terribly seriously. But once you get deep into it, you not only hurt yourself, but you hurt everyone around you."

They ate the rest of their breakfast in silence.

Cassandra finally got up, coming out fully made-up and primped as if she were going out to an exclusive nightclub, and had a bite of toast before leaving. She said nothing more than was required.

Good Lord, Della thought. *Is she going to be like this the entire trip?*

Sebastian picked up a rental car he had hired and got behind the wheel since he was the only one who knew where they were going. They quickly passed beyond the little houses and shops of Kirkwall and into an open countryside of rolling green hills under a slate-gray sky. The rain was holding off, at least.

Those three brief yet vivid dreams remained stuck in Della's head, as clear as when she had woken up. She desperately wanted to talk to the others about it, but not with Sebastian present. He had a long way to go before he would take something like that seriously.

They weren't far out of town before Della felt a pulse of energy. She glanced at Lucas and Richard, who both gave her knowing looks to show they had felt it too. A ley line, and a strong one. Cassandra did not acknowledge them, but Della could see her looking out the window, her pert features set in concentration.

The only one who appeared oblivious was Sebastian.

A few miles later, they passed across another ley line and felt another pulse of energy. The lines of power hadn't felt this strong down south.

"How are you feeling, Sebastian?" Della asked right after they passed over the second line.

"Fine. Richard's hangover cure is deservedly famous."

That's not what I meant. "No, I mean, you jerked in your seat just now."

"Did I?"

No, I'm just fishing for information.

Sebastian shrugged and didn't say anything.

The road led them through farmland for twenty minutes or so before they caught the first glints of the sea off to their left. Rain beaded on the window. Della stared ahead, feeling something strange shift within her. The road turned inland again. Up ahead she could make out the stone circle—a few tall, thin rectangles black against the gray sky. Beyond it, dull under the leaden sky, were the waters of a loch.

"We're almost there," Della said.

"Oh, that's not the Ring of Brodgar," Sebastian said. "Those are the Standing Stones of Stenness. The Ring of Brodgar is another mile farther on. We can park here and walk the rest of the way if you want to look at both of them. It's beginning to rain, though."

The road curved a little in line with the shore, and suddenly, they were driving right for the stone circle, still a half a mile in the distance.

As the road curved, Della felt the jolt of another ley line. This time, the feeling didn't go away. They were driving right along it, and from what little she had learned about how ley lines worked, it would cut straight through the nearest stone circle and lead directly to the Ring of Brodgar.

"I think we should park and walk," Della said, her voice breaking. With trembling hands, she zipped up her raincoat and put on her hood.

"I agree," Cassandra said. She sounded somewhat flustered. It was the first time she had spoken since they had left the rental flat.

"Are you sure?" Sebastian asked. "The rain is picking up."

"Park and we'll walk," Della said.

There was a small pullout by the road, and he stopped the car.

They stepped out, and Della felt the power of the ley lines overcome her.

Everything went black.

11

THE POWER THROBBING through the ley lines almost knocked Lucas over. He leaned against the car, hands cradling his head, as a wave of dizziness came over him. Dimly he heard someone shouting.

The moment passed. Sebastian was leaning over Della, who had fallen to her knees on the gravel pullout by the road. Richard and Cassandra stood nearby, unsteady on their feet.

In the few seconds it took for Sebastian to get Della to her feet and lead her back to the car, Lucas had recovered.

The power passing through the ley line remained like the throb of a great engine, shaking him to his core.

He moved over to his two friends, careful on his feet so he didn't fall over like Della had.

"What the hell was that?" he asked in a low voice. He needn't have bothered. Sebastian was fussing loudly over Della, who kept insisting that nothing was wrong, that she was just tired and had become dizzy.

She knows better than that, Lucas thought. *But it's best to keep the ex-boyfriend in the dark for the time being. He needs to be brought in slowly.*

"The power coming through this line is immense," Cassandra said, still looking a bit pale. "Every Sensitive on the islands must be feeling this."

"I nearly fell over like Della did," Lucas said.

"We would have, too, if we hadn't any training," Richard said.

"So what's going on?" Lucas asked. He could feel the taint in the power and knew they could too.

Cassandra and Richard glanced at each other, unsure.

"We need to do a ritual to get to the bottom of this," Cassandra said.

"Not with Sebastian here," Lucas said.

"No. We'll have to ditch him tonight," Richard said, studying the classics student as he leaned into the car, speaking to Della. He had put her in there to keep her out of the rain. "Funny he doesn't seem to be affected. I'm sure I'm feeling the Talent in him."

"I do too," Cassandra said. "And you mentioned that he managed to scare off both Wayland the Smith and Old Mother Shipton."

"Well, temporarily scared them off. They smacked him about a moment later. But yes, no one could hold them off for even a second without some innate ability."

"So why isn't it manifesting now?" Lucas asked.

"Another puzzle. What's this?"

A car pulled up behind theirs. Bjorn stepped out, wearing a heavy blue coat and black cap instead of the raincoats they all wore. Lucas thought he looked like a sailor.

"Hello!" the Dane said in a cheery tone. "I was driving to the Ring of Brodgar and spotted you. I was going to show you this after the Ring of Brodgar, but the other way around will do just as well."

"Hello, Bjorn," Sebastian called, not leaving Della's side. "Della's not feeling too well."

She managed a weak smile. "Oh, it's nothing. Just a bit of dizziness. I had a long day yesterday and didn't get much sleep."

Della got up, gently removed Sebastian's helping

hand, squared her shoulders, and said, "I'm fine now. Let's take a look at these stones."

Bjorn offered his arm, which she took.

"Careful on this grass. It gets slippery in a light rain like this."

Frowning, Lucas followed. The others fell in behind.

"So, what do you know about this place?" Bjorn asked.

"It's a henge monument, a ditched enclosure with a stone circle inside," Della said. "One of the oldest in the world. From 3100 BC, I think."

"That's right. There were originally a dozen of these stones, but now, as you can see, there are only four."

That hasn't lessened their power, Lucas thought. The pulsing of the ley line increased as they drew closer to the circle. Della's steps wavered a bit, and Bjorn clutched on her arm.

"Careful, I told you this grass is slippery. If I didn't know better, I would think you outdrank those three guys last night."

"Watch out for Richard. He'll lay you out if you're not careful."

"Oh, I'm Danish. I can handle it."

They came to the stones, four tall slabs, the

biggest standing more than twice the height of a man. Low stones had been set by the modern care-takers to show where the originals had been. Lucas walked to the center of the circle, feeling the power growing beneath his feet.

"Careful," Richard said. He had joined him. Cassandra and Sebastian stood by Bjorn, who spoke only to Della.

Lucas turned to look down the ley line as it ran straight to the Ring of Brodgar, a more complete stone circle just visible in the distance at the other end of a thin spit of land cutting between two lochs. Even if he had been blindfolded, he would have known where the other stone circle stood. The power of the line was so strong it felt like he was standing on a live wire.

Bjorn continued talking, utterly unaware of the massive energies beneath his feet.

"There are some interesting stories relating to these two stone circles. The Orcadians called this the Temple of the Moon while they called the Ring of Brodgar the Temple of the Sun."

"Are there any astronomical alignments to support that theory?" Della asked, trying to regain her composure. "Many stone circles have them."

"I don't know much about that," Bjorn admitted.

"It's not really my specialty. But I do know of one such alignment. See that tall stone by the road just where the land narrows before leading to the Ring of Brodgar? That's called the Watchstone."

It was one of a pair, Lucas thought. *And they were two of several pairs.*

Lucas didn't know how he knew this, only that he did.

"It was originally one of a pair," Bjorn said. "The other was on the other side of the road. It was a symbolic gateway between the two stone circles. Some archaeologists theorize there was a series of such gateways running to the Ring of Brodgar."

"That makes sense," Della said in a quiet voice. "Yes, I think there were."

She feels it too, Lucas thought.

"Now, see that distant hill? If you stand at the Watchstone during sunset at the winter solstice, you're at the perfect angle to spot something interesting, weather permitting. The sun will set behind that hill, moving at a sharp angle since we're so far north. Now see how that hill has a steep side and then another smaller hill to the right of it? As the sun angles farther toward the horizon, it reappears for a minute before setting behind that smaller hill."

"The sun is reborn," Lucas said. "That's the

promise of midwinter solstice, that the shortest day of the year will see longer days after it. Ancient peoples thought of it as the sun being reborn."

"That's right," Sebastian's Danish friend said before turning back to Della. "Now, you were interested in the local folklore. These two stone circles were associated with an interesting custom until the beginning of the nineteenth century. For five days starting at New Year, people would come from all over the islands to have a big party. Of course, the unmarried boys and girls would all get to flirting. You didn't get much socializing in those days, especially if you were in some isolated farmhouse or hamlet."

"Sounds peaceful," Della said.

"Try spending the winter here! So, some of the boys and girls would like each other, and since they might not see each other again until the next year, they promised themselves to one another right then and there. They'd slip away from the festivities at night and come here. The girl would kneel down and swear an oath to Odin to be true to her man."

"Odin? Really?" Cassandra asked.

"Oh yes, the Norse tradition is strong in the northern islands, even more so in Shetland and the Faroes than here. Once the girl made her oath, the couple would then go to the Ring of Brodgar, and the man would kneel down and make the same oath. After that, they'd come back here to a stone that used to stand right over there. It was called Odin's Stone and had a hole in it."

Bjorn took a step back from Della. "There was a hole in that stone, and the man and woman would reach through it and take each other's hands." He reached for Della, who took his hand. "And that made the promise sacrosanct. They were as good as married. All that was left was to arrange it between the two families."

Della was no longer pale. In fact, she was blushing.

"So, what happened to Odin's Stone?" she asked.

"Some incomer—that's the term for someone who moves to the island from elsewhere—owned this land and didn't like young couples in love stomping all over it, so he tore the Odin Stone down and broke it into pieces."

"That couldn't have been popular."

"They tried to burn down his house."

Della laughed. "Good for them!"

They were still holding hands.

Lucas cleared his throat. "Fascinating. Shall we move on to the Ring of Brodgar?"

Bjorn turned to Lucas. Their eyes met, and a small smile crept over the Dane's lips.

"Whatever you want."

He held Della's hand a moment longer before releasing it. "I'll drive you up there, if you like," Bjorn told her.

I suppose none of us are invited, Lucas thought.

"Oh, let's walk. The rain isn't so bad," Della said.

"You're turning into an islander already!" Bjorn said. They headed out onto the spit of land leading to the larger stone circle, seemingly unaware, and uncaring, whether the rest followed.

Sebastian caught up with them and started talking to Bjorn about some mutual acquaintance. The rest of the group hung back.

"I've never felt the lines this strong," Richard said.

"Tainted too." Cassandra wrinkled her nose. She seemed to have gotten out of her sulk now that there was work to do.

"Isn't this what those books were talking about? A taint in the ley lines that the lines themselves would eventually fix?" Lucas asked, forcing himself to concentrate on the job.

"Exactly," Richard replied. "That's why the local mage's circle wanted those books, in order to protect themselves against this. But why is this happening? And how could they have predicted it?"

Lucas had no answers to those questions. All he knew was that they would have to do another ritual to find out more, and considering the state of the ley lines, and the proximity of a powerful circle of mages, that was going to be seriously dangerous.

"Have you studied those rituals yourself?" Cassandra asked. "Can we protect ourselves if we can't stop it before it's too late?"

Richard nodded somberly. "Yes, I read through those books enough that I could protect us, but do you want to live in a world where everyone has been turned to ash?"

Cassandra didn't have an answer to that.

Lucas looked at Sebastian, tagging along with Bjorn and Della like an unwanted puppy. They'd have to do the ritual behind his back somehow. As eager as he had suddenly become, the classics student was still an outsider. If magical practitioners had learned anything in the past two thousand years, it was that outsiders were dangerous. Lucas hadn't wanted him along in the first place.

They approached the Ring of Brodgar, standing right at the opposite end of the spit of land dividing the two lochs. It was a stunning sight. Like the

Standing Stones of Stenness, the stone circle was made up of tall, thin slabs, not the thick heavy stones of stone circles in England. The overcast sky, the rain, and the surrounding heather around these grim, gray stones all conspired to create an atmosphere of quiet power. A wind blew across the water of the two lochs, making Lucas zip up his coat to the neck.

The stones were smaller than those of the other circle—the height of a man or a bit taller—but there were more of them, creating a complete circle that they now entered. This place, he knew, was one of the largest stone circles in the British Isles, and certainly one of the most powerful in earth energy. Lucas's skin prickled as the power beneath him increased with every step.

He studied Sebastian. He did not seem affected at all. Was he really a Sensitive like Richard thought?

Bjorn started up his lecture to Della again. Lucas listened in, although it was obvious the Dane didn't care whether or not anyone else heard.

"I've already told you the most famous bit of folk-lore regarding this place, and now I want to show you my favorite little detail."

He led them to one of the stones and placed his finger on the worn, wet surface.

Everyone gathered around. Lucas could make out Nordic runes carved on the surface.

"Bjorn," Richard said. "It's faint, but that's definitely your name."

Bjorn laughed. "I'm surprised you can read runic!"

"I have more surprises than that," Richard said, smiling.

"Um, yes. Well, there are more Norse runes. On this stone over here is a cross. It was probably carved by the Norse after they converted to Christianity. It's too faint and weathered to be more modern. Some people say it was to break the power of a pagan monument, but the Vikings were more flexible than that. They incorporated the old ways and the new, just like later generations of Orcadians were strong Christians but kept many pagan practices. Now here's another one."

He led them across the circle, their boots swishing through the wet heather, to one of the tallest stones. Lucas and Richard exchanged glances. This one broadcast power like a radio transmitter.

"What do you see here?" Bjorn asked.

Sebastian was the first to spot it. "An anvil," he said, his voice shaking.

"Yes, it is. You have sharp eyes, old friend."

Sebastian licked his lips. "Is that a symbol of... Wayland the Smith?"

"Most likely, yes. I'm surprised a classics student would know that."

"I've... been exposed to the legend."

Bjorn nodded, oblivious. "This is what I was saying. The Norse incorporated their old gods and their new faith without feeling any sense of contradiction. Plus, they took over existing sacred sites in the places they conquered. Wayland's anvil appears on many of the stones scattered around the northern isles. I've seen them on menhirs as far north as Shetland and on natural rocks in the Faroe Islands. Lots of hammers, too, which are generally interpreted as symbolizing Thor but might be Wayland instead."

Sebastian was no longer listening. He was walking away on unsteady feet.

"What's the matter?" Bjorn asked at his receding back.

"He's not feeling well," Della said.

"That makes two of you. I hope you didn't get food poisoning from the airline meal."

"He'll be all right," Lucas said, although he didn't think that was true. "Tell us more. This is very helpful."

"Well, Della here was interested in astronomical

alignments. Strangely, there is only one probable one for the Ring of Brodgar, but that might be because some of the stones are missing and we can't see the whole pattern."

More likely because this is the power center for the entire network of northern ley lines and it has more important things to do than tell a bunch of puny humans when to plant their crops, Lucas thought.

"What about that outlier over there?" Della asked, pointing to a modest stone of about five feet in height more than a hundred yards away.

Bjorn grinned. "Ah! You have a good eye. That's it. I can see why you took up archaeology."

Della beamed. Lucas rolled his eyes.

"That's called the Comet Stone, although most likely that name is a modern invention. In the old days, it was called the Oil Stone. Nobody knows why. But locals used to doff their hats when they passed by."

"Interesting," Richard said. "I think I'll go over and have a better look."

"There's nothing much to see. You won't find my name in runic, in any case. But if you stand there at sunset during the spring or autumn equinoxes, you'll see the sun touch the most westerly stones of the ring. If it isn't raining, that is. The

Orkney Islands aren't the best place to do astronomy."

Della looked back at the spit of land leading to the Standing Stones of Stenness, their tall stones looming in the distance. She was looking right along the ley line.

"These two stone circles make such a beautiful symmetry," she murmured. "And look how the hills all around put this whole place in a sort of bowl. I've read that this valley is full of Neolithic sites. It's odd that the Ring of Brodgar, the most impressive monument here, was the last one built. It didn't get completed until 2000 BC, a thousand years after the other stone circle."

Bjorn smiled. "That's right. You know your onions, as the English say." The two of them laughed.

Are they going to be like this all day? Lucas fumed.

12

DELLA WAS HAVING an amazing day with Bjorn. He was so friendly, so knowledgeable about things she found interesting, that he put her immediately at ease. That was rare in any situation and doubly so for the situation she found herself in at the moment. The stress of feeling such tainted earth energy wherever she went was wearing on her. He talked to her about magic and otherworldly beings like they were simple constructions of premodern culture, not the real and dangerous entities that she knew them to be. It took her mind off things a bit, reassured her.

He was attentive too. Della had always been the quiet, studious type, easily overlooked by extroverts like Bjorn. But he made an effort to listen and didn't need to feign an interest in her accounts of excavations in the United States and England. He enjoyed the folktales she had learned related to the Rollright Stones near Oxford. She skipped the part about the legends of the witch Old Mother Shipton being true, however. She didn't want him thinking she was some lunatic.

Instead she kept up an easy banter that ranged from intellectual conversation to enthusiastic sightseeing to subtle flirting.

She kept a part of her mind in reserve, however, as she always did. While she allowed herself to relax and go with the flow of conversation, the aloof, analytical part of her studied everything Bjorn said to find anything that might be of use.

Because the unsettling power crackling through the ley line beneath them would not make her forget her mission completely. No, not for an instant. An awesome guy like Bjorn only made it a bit more tolerable.

After studying the Ring of Brodgar, they retreated back to the cars in an increasingly heavy rain and drove to Maeshowe. Della rode in Bjorn's car, and the conversation continued uninterrupted.

"So, you're quite the research team," Bjorn said.

"We're a motley crew, that's for sure."

"Why are you coming up here in the winter and during term? Wouldn't summer be better?"

Della shifted in her seat at this awkward question. Their cover story didn't make much sense from an academic point of view. It was the best they could come up with, though, if they wanted his assistance.

"We were... busy during the summer." Della hated to lie to this guy, yet she didn't see how she had much choice. She decided to lie as little as possible. "I was working on an excavation at the Rollright Stones, like I said, plus doing a lot of lab work. Lucas and Cassandra and Richard were doing research in London. And as you know, Sebastian was in Greece."

Bjorn looked at her sidelong. "Sebastian mentioned you."

Her heart did a flip-flop. "Did he?"

"Yeah. He mentioned he had a new girlfriend, an archaeology student from America. I felt sorry for him."

"Excuse me?"

Bjorn shrugged. "Most of his friends figured out how he was. We never brought it up because he never did. It was obvious, though."

Della crossed her arms. "It wasn't obvious to me."

He glanced at her again from the corner of his eye. "So, he didn't talk to you about it?"

"Not exactly, no."

"So you guys have broken up."

"Oh, hell yes."

"Then why are you two still doing a project together? Sorry if I'm prying. He's an old friend. I worry about him."

"It's... complicated."

"That's cool that you two managed to stay friends."

Sort of. "Yeah."

"You guys seeing other people now?"

Della's heart did another flip-flop, for a different reason this time. "No. I'm single! Um, I mean, I'm not seeing anyone. I don't think he is either."

"That's great! I'll ask him out tonight."

Della stared at him.

A grin crept across his face, and he suddenly burst out laughing. "Got you."

Della laughed too. After their laughter faded away, they fell into an easy silence. The car sped along a narrow road through open fields of heather. To their right lay the loch, dull and flat in the rain. Della glanced in Bjorn's direction and caught him looking at her. They gave each other brief smiles but said nothing.

"What's that?" Bjorn asked after a minute.

Two cars sat motionless in the lane ahead, both at an awkward angle and nose to nose with each other. Two people, a man and a woman, stood by the shoulder.

"Looks like an accident," Della said. "I hope no one's hurt."

Bjorn slowed to pass. The fronts of both cars were crumpled, and there was a scattering of broken plastic and glass from the headlights on the road. When he saw no cars coming in the opposite direction, he stopped and rolled down the window.

"Everyone all right?"

"Yes, no thanks to this idiot!" a woman snapped.

"I told you, I saw a child run across the street," the man said.

"And where is he?" The woman put her arms out to encompass the surrounding area, which was flat all around.

"I don't know. All I saw was a child in a red cap run across the road. He or she must be around here somewhere."

"Maybe you should look for him at the bottom of

whatever bottle you drained before getting behind the wheel!"

"I haven't been drinking."

Bjorn drove off. The two didn't even notice. They were too busy arguing.

"Good thing he didn't drive into us," Bjorn said.

Della didn't know what to say. She peered at the dwindling scene through the rearview mirror.

A large, grassy mound appeared by the side of the road. Bjorn pulled off into a small, abandoned parking lot.

"Here already?" Della asked. She had been hoping for a longer drive.

"Yes, only three miles away from the Standing Stones of Stenness. There's a whole cluster of ancient sites around here, all within easy walking distance of each other, at least if it isn't a cold, rainy day. You should really come up here in summer. It can be beautiful, and the day lasts almost all night."

"Sounds nice." It did, but Della was distracted by the strong energy radiating off the burial mound. Even though they weren't parked on the ley line— estimating by where the stone circles stood, she judged that the ley line just missed the parking lot— she could still feel the energy.

Della didn't think that was normal. She had

never felt the energy of a sacred site before actually being in contact with it.

"There are some wonderful hikes," Bjorn went on. "You can even take a boat to some of the smaller islands that are completely uninhabited. All that's there now are fulmars and puffins."

The other car pulled in beside them. Della saw Lucas looking at her through the window and turned back to Bjorn.

"Before you show me the puffins, show me Maeshowe."

"I'd be glad to. And this evening I'd like to show you some of Kirkwall's nightlife."

Della, flustered, didn't answer. The others were already piling out of their car, so she used that as an excuse to put the hood of her raincoat over her head and open the door to join them.

"You all right?" Lucas asked in a low voice. Both Sebastian and Bjorn were still turning off their engines.

"Yeah. I can feel it from here."

Lucas nodded. "Be careful you don't faint like before. The last place nearly knocked me over too. This is the center. I can feel it."

The two drivers got out of their cars, and he turned away from her.

"All right," Bjorn said, facing the group like a tour guide. "This is Maeshowe, and as our archaeologist could tell us, it's one of the most impressive Neolithic chambered cairns in the world. It was finished around 2700 BC, so between the times of the two stone circles we just saw."

"Can we get inside?" Richard asked, staring at the mound. There was a modern steel door, tightly shut, blocking off a rock-lined cutting into the side of the mound. No one else was in sight.

Bjorn held up a key. "Yes, we can. As part of my work-study arrangement with the university, I work as a tour guide for this area. I do have to sell you tickets for that. Sorry, I'd let you in for free, but I'm not allowed. I'll take your money at the office we have just inside."

He led them toward the mound. It was one of the biggest she'd ever seen, well over a hundred feet in diameter, a dull green hill beneath a gloomy sky. Della braced herself for the power she knew she would feel as soon as she stepped within the confines of the burial mound.

It hit her earlier than she expected and nearly bowled her over.

Bjorn walked a bit ahead, unaware, but as she looked around, she saw everyone else except Sebastian go pale and stumble a little. Sebastian looked at the others curiously but said nothing.

There must have been a ditch around this place, enclosing the sacred precinct. A lot of burial mounds had them. So we're already inside the site.

Della glanced up at the mound looming above her and remembered her dream of Montague pouring beer inside a mound much like this, although smaller and with no obvious entrance.

What was it he'd said?

"You have to give them some, but take care not to give them too much."

What could that mean? She needed to talk with the others about that. Plus those other two dreams she had.

If only she could find a time without Sebastian around. As helpful as he had turned out to be, she found his presence suffocating. It would have been better to visit here without him. Then she and the others could have spoken freely.

Bjorn went to the steel door, which he unlocked and opened with a loud creak. He flicked on a light, and they saw before them a long, low, stone-lined passageway leading into the mound's dark interior. The floor was made up of huge flagstones that must have weighed several tons each.

Della trembled, both from the cold air outside and from a spiritual cold she felt emanating from within.

"Welcome to the ticket office," Bjorn said with a chuckle. A small shelf by the door held a cashbox, a ledger, and a book of tickets.

They paid, a mundane act that seemed surreal in the face of the arcane powers reverberating all around them. Bjorn chattered away about his work with the tourism bureau, still completely unaware of the hidden forces in this ancient place.

I was like that once, Della thought with a pang. *Not so long ago.*

She looked down the passage, trying to guess what might lie within. If it was like the other chambered cairns she'd been in, this passage, barely three feet high, would lead to a large central chamber with smaller side chambers. People would have been buried in each room. In many of these tombs, archaeologists had found evidence that they were reopened periodically, with more human remains placed inside. These had already been "defleshed," as the archaeological euphemism went, meaning they had been left for the crows to pick clean. Once enough bones were gathered over a few years, the tomb would be ritually reopened, and a pile of new bones would be stacked upon the old.

Aunt Mary had talked about how magic often had a flavor. If a certain sacred spot was used for a certain type of rite, then it would be more attuned to that sort of magic.

No prizes for what kind of magic can be cast in this place, Della thought with a shudder.

Bjorn must have noticed, because he cocked his head and gave her a reassuring smile. "Afraid of the dark?"

I didn't used to be.

It was Richard who answered. "This girl isn't afraid of anything. She's a warrior through and through."

Della smiled, although his words did not reassure her. Yes, she had become a warrior of a sort. That didn't stop her from being terrified.

Bjorn flicked another light, and the passage lit up. At the end, they could just make out a larger chamber. Bjorn led them down the passage, everyone having to crouch and take care not to bash their heads on the low ceiling.

After an uncomfortable walk, Richard complaining about his back the whole way, they came to a large, vaulted chamber.

Everyone stood and stared in wonder. The chamber was made up of flat stones stacked on top of one another in an overlapping pattern without any mortar, each stone fitted cleverly so that no mortar was needed to make a structure that would survive the centuries. Each wall had a small passage that Bjorn told them led to a side chamber where additional burials would have been.

Then he began to point out the Norse runes scratched, no doubt with the tips of swords or daggers, onto the stones that made up the wall. He read some aloud. "'Ofram the son of Sigurd carved these runes.' 'Ingigerth is the most beautiful of all women.' 'He is a Viking... come here under the barrow.'"

Bjorn moved to another wall and pointed at a longer inscription. "Here's the one I told you about: 'Crusaders broke into Maeshowe. Lif the earl's cook carved these runes. To the northwest is a great treasure hidden. It was long ago that a great treasure was hidden here. Happy is he that might find that great treasure. Hakon alone bore treasure from this mound.' It's signed by someone called 'Simon Sirith.'"

"That's an odd name for a Norseman," Richard said.

Bjorn nodded. "It is. Simon is a Biblical name, so that might explain it. These were men who had volunteered for the Crusades. Christians. The last name is odd, too, though."

"A foreigner?" Della asked.

"Perhaps." Bjorn shrugged. "People got around. The Vikings took slaves from all parts of the northern world and the Mediterranean too. Plus, some hardy merchants and other travelers sailed around this region."

"I'm surprised he didn't sign in his own language," Della said.

"Well, he had lived with the Norse long enough to know their writing system, although for a literate man, that wouldn't have taken long to learn. It's just another alphabet. Perhaps he wanted to fit in with his companions. Plus, he would want what he had written to be read by those who came after."

"It's just strange somehow..." Della felt faint again. The power in this place was almost overwhelming her, and the taint she could feel in it made her nauseous.

And that feeling was growing.

She rested a hand on the wall to steady herself.

"Careful," Bjorn said. "You don't want to touch any of the runes."

Della ignored him, looking around at the others. Sebastian was staring at her, his face lined with concern, while the rest—Lucas, Richard, and Cassandra—were glancing all around them.

They looked terrified.

Then she noticed something else.

It was getting warmer.

While the dank, quiet interior had been cool when they had entered, now it felt more like room temperature.

"Doesn't it feel warm in here?" Sebastian asked.

"Yeah," Bjorn said, looking around curiously. "I've had bigger groups than this in here, and it didn't warm up."

So it really is room temperature, Della thought. *Not some spiritual trick I'd have to endure a lecture from Richard or Cassandra to understand.*

Della, her head spinning, her voice husky, said, "I think something's wrong. Richard, should we—"

She never got to finish her question, because just then sparks sputtered out of the wiring next to the lone light bulb in the wall, and all went dark.

The nausea Della had been feeling washed over her stronger than before. She doubled over, clenching her stomach. If she hadn't been holding onto the wall, she felt sure she would have fallen over. Distantly she heard her companions shouting.

Someone pulled out a cell phone, the light from its screen barely cutting through the stygian darkness.

The wires next to the bulb sparked again.

"We got to get out of here!" Bjorn shouted. "I need to switch off the mains power outside."

Another cell phone switched on, whoever was holding it having the presence of mind to turn on the flashlight function and beam it at the exit. Strangely, the light did not penetrate as much as it should. It looked as if it were shining through thick gauze.

"Smoke!" Bjorn shouted, although Della smelled no smoke. "Hurry."

They made for the exit. The low, cramped passage forced them to go one by one. Everyone seemed to move slowly, as if in a dream. Della found herself at the back of the line, trailing behind as the others struggled through the dim light, hunched over and breathing heavily.

And that was when she felt rough hands grab her from the shadows behind.

Della stumbled and tried to tear out of their grasp, but as she was bent over in the cramped tunnel, she didn't have much leverage. The hands got her in a tight grip. There were several of them—too many—grabbing her raincoat by the tail. More grabbed her shoulders and waist. How could so many people fit behind her in such a small tunnel? She tried to cry out but only managed a strangled, choking sound.

She fell to her knees. The others rushed on ahead, the lights from their cell phones dimming in the distance, leaving her in ever-deepening shadow. Behind her lay only darkness.

Her unseen assailants pulled at her, causing her to tip over and slap her hands flat on the flagstones to keep from smashing her face.

That was when she saw the hands holding her.

They were small but gave the appearance of great strength. As far as she could make out in the dim light, the skin was greenish gray, warty, and rough. The fingers ended in long black nails that tore at her raincoat.

And there were so many of them. At least a dozen. It was impossible that so many could fit in the passageway behind her, but she didn't dare look to see how they did it.

They started pulling her back, back into the bowels of the Stone Age tomb, back into the darkness, away from her swiftly receding friends.

Della slid backward along the ancient flagstones. In panic she grabbed onto the walls on either side of the passageway, her fingers finding purchase on the rough stone.

For a moment, she stopped. The hands tightened their grip, pulling harder. Her fingers strained then gave way.

She slid back, ever faster, into the depths of the tomb.

13

LUCAS WAS the second to last in line fleeing the Maeshowe tomb, and he had almost made it out when he realized Della was no longer behind him.

Bjorn slid the bolt on the door and opened it. Lucas blinked at the daylight. Even though it was a rainy day in the far north, the daylight still stung his eyes after the near darkness of their flight from the tomb. He gave the view of the outside world one longing look and turned back to find Della.

But not before grabbing Richard, who was right ahead of him, spinning him around, and hauling him back with him.

"Ow!" his friend protested. "You made me hit my... oh."

"We have to find her!"

"There's only one place she can be," Richard said as they retraced their steps in the bobbing light of Lucas's mobile phone. "Assuming they haven't taken her to another plane of existence yet."

Lucas didn't know how that could be possible and didn't have time to think on it. They rushed forward, Lucas crying out as he bumped his head on a low stone, and came to the main chamber...

...just in time to see Della get dragged into one of the side burial chambers.

Richard pulled an amulet out of his pocket, the same one he had used to face the fire spirit. He began shouting in Medieval Latin. Lucas plunged into the side chamber.

It was a cramped, dank little place, not much bigger than a walk-in closet, yet the flashlight on his phone barely illuminated it.

Della lay on the floor, thrashing against a cluster of gauzy black shadows that writhed around her and closed on her arms and legs. Focusing his spiritual will, Lucas reached for the closest shadow and tried to grasp it.

Instead of passing through the thing as if it were smoke as he half expected to, his hand clenched on something cold and rough, a physical thing he could not see. He yanked with all his might, using his willpower as much as his considerable strength, and managed to pull it off Della.

The force of it coming unstuck from his friend threw him backward. His back hit hard against the rough wall, the corner of one stone jabbing the small of his back, and he fell. The thing fell right on top of him...

...and materialized.

It was a squat, greenish-gray creature in old-style homespun and a pointed red woolen cap. Lucas could not tell if that ugly face belonged to a man or woman.

The thing snarled at him, showing yellow teeth.

Lucas cried out and punched... it. It fell to one side. Lucas pushed to his knees then got thrown back down immediately as the creature barreled into his chest. He could hear Richard still shouting in Latin. Out of the corner of his eye, he saw Della struggling with several of the creatures, now changed from shadows into something terrifyingly real, and that was all he saw.

He was too busy fighting for his life.

The thing knelt on his chest, bony knees grinding into his gut as those taloned hands reached for his throat.

Lucas batted them away and bucked, trying to

get the thing off him. The creature—*troll*, Lucas realized with horror—changed tactics and grabbed onto the front of his raincoat. Now it stuck to him no matter how much he writhed and dodged.

The troll tried to bite his throat.

Lucas managed to clamp a hand on the thing's face and push it away in time, but it did not relax its grip on his raincoat.

Three punches in quick succession with his free hand took care of that. It fell to the ground, stood up to its somehow intimidating full height of three feet, and pulled a greasy little chicken bone out of its pocket.

Lucas did not wait to see what kind of old magic that might be. Still on the ground, he lifted up both feet and kicked the thing across the chamber. It hit the far wall with a loud thud and fell to the floor.

He didn't have time to see if the thing recovered. Della was still fighting for her life against half a dozen of them, and something strange was happening to her.

She seemed to be fading.

He plunged into the fray, trying to grasp a couple of the trolls that were on her, but unlike with his previous opponent, he had a hard time gripping or even seeing them.

They're trying to take her into their world. The scene in the burial chamber began to fade. *Oh no, they're trying to take me too!*

He realized the power coming off of Richard's spell was the only thing keeping them there.

But for how long?

He continued trying to pry the trolls off Della, but it was like fighting the wind. Fatigue set in, a sleepiness that no amount of terror could stop. He felt himself losing the will to fight. In the distance, he thought he could hear faint music, some merry folk song played on a fiddle and flute. The room around him continued to fade, and he found he did not care much. So what if they took him? Would that be so bad? The music lulled him. He could go listen. He could join in the dance.

All he had to do was let go.

His tenuous grip on the spirits, and reality, slipped.

A shock jerked him awake. He thought Della might have shouted, but he was not sure if she had screamed with her voice or her spirit. He found himself on the floor. The burial chamber had grown brighter, but still there floated dark wisps of shadow that writhed around him and his two friends. Della lay on the floor, propped up on one elbow and waving her free hand at the apparitions. Richard continued to intone in Latin.

Summoning up his will, Lucas struggled to his feet. The force of the three of them united made the shadows fade and finally wink out.

Lucas did not stop to question how exactly they had been saved. He grabbed Della and headed out of the room, Richard taking up the rear, his amulet still held aloft.

They raced through the main chamber and headed for the exit.

They came upon Cassandra heading back inside.

"You all right?" she asked.

"All right enough," Lucas said, all but pushing her aside in his rush to get away. "Let's get out of here!"

They stumbled outside. A hard rain from a gray sky had never looked so beautiful to him. Bjorn stood in the rain talking on his phone not too far away. He turned to give them a concerned, then relieved, look. Sebastian stood uncertainly nearby. When he saw them emerge, he hurried over.

"What happened?"

If you had come to help, you would have seen for yourself, Lucas fumed. "Della bumped her head in the dark. She'll be all right."

"Looks like you did too," Sebastian said, pointing.

Lucas reached up to the throbbing pain in his forehead that he hadn't had time to think about before and, when he pulled his hand away, saw blood. The rain soon washed it away.

But it could not wash away the memory of what they had seen in there.

They kept moving, heading for the cars, not knowing and not caring what Bjorn thought of all this. Only Cassandra, ever worried about perceptions, stopped to talk with him. Lucas was in such a hurry to drive away that he almost left her behind.

An hour later, Lucas lay collapsed on his bed, emotionally, physically, and spiritually drained. The tension of the day, the taint of the dark forces he had had to endure for hours, the fight, and that irritating Dane all conspired to sap his energy.

Funny he should think of him when he had just faced a crowd of trolls. Some Aryan überfolklorist was the least of his worries.

They were back at the rental flat, all of them as drained as he was except for Della, who, while obviously as affected by the magic as anyone, had been sunny throughout the day—except for when they were visiting the sites themselves.

He had even heard her trading numbers with

Bjorn before they went into Maeshowe.

Bah! At least he was out of their hair for a while. Sebastian had stayed with Bjorn to meet up with the emergency services and then called to say he was taking him out for a pint. The sun had already set. It was barely five, and Lucas felt like he could sleep until morning. They really should be taking advantage of Sebastian's absence to conduct a scrying ritual, but none of them had the strength. They were lucky to still be breathing.

Or to still be here at all, Lucas thought with a shudder. *Those things tried to take us away.*

Despite the fear, his fatigue got the better of him. He was just drifting off to sleep when there came a tentative knock on the door.

"Come in," he said in a tone that hopefully would send the caller away.

It did not.

Della opened the door a crack.

"Are you asleep?" she asked.

Not anymore.

"Just resting my eyes. Come on in."

She came in quietly and, to his surprise, closed the door behind her and sat on the edge of his bed. Lucas felt a warm flush go through him. He hadn't had a woman sit on his bed since... well... Cassandra.

He immediately put the spoiled rich girl out of his thoughts.

"What's on your mind?" he asked after she had sat there a moment, looking at the floor.

"I had some dreams last night. There wasn't a chance to tell you before because Sebastian was around."

"What kind of dreams?"

She proceeded to tell him. As he listened, he sat up then stood and started pacing the room. These were important. Very important. He knew he should call the others in, but he didn't want to deal with them right now. Somehow it felt nice to have this awkward Yank confiding only in him.

Once she finished, he sat back down beside her. As he did, he realized he had sat a bit too close for courtesy. He didn't move away since that would only highlight what he had done. She didn't move away either, no doubt because she was too preoccupied by her visions.

"The dream about Montague must have been him trying to communicate," Lucas said.

"But why not speak to us directly?"

"Maybe he can't. Communication with the spiritual world is tricky and often indirect. That time he appeared to us during the ritual in his house, for most of the contact he was speaking to himself, not us, yet at the same time he was giving us information we needed."

"About him missing something. I've been wondering about that."

"So have I. He seemed to be confused as to why he hadn't gone completely to the other side. I think he felt he had something he needed to do first, something on this plane of existence that he didn't manage to complete before he died."

"Like pouring half a pint of beer into the top of a burial mound?"

Lucas smiled. That old skepticism was back. He understood now that it was a defense mechanism. No one could be in denial after what had happened at Maeshowe. He found it endearing. "Perhaps not literally. I'm sure you know of the practice of leaving offerings to the trolls or fairies who were believed to live in the mounds."

"Yeah. You get that all over northern Europe."

"And we have just seen that the epicenter of the taint in the ley lines is at a burial mound."

"I didn't see Maeshowe in my dream. I saw a much smaller burial mound."

"Yes, but it's more symbolic than literal. Give them just enough but not too much. That's what he was telling us. But what could it mean? That's what I don't understand."

"What do you think of the little girl with the crow's head?"

"No idea. I don't know why she was being scolded either."

"The woman with the rocks on her at the beach looked like some sort of ritual."

"Perhaps an initiation."

Della snapped her fingers. "Right! The beach is a liminal space. With the tides, sometimes it's land and sometimes it's sea. It's neither one nor the other, so it's a good place for sacred rituals and magic. You see that all over the ancient world. The Romans had protective gods for doorways, because it was neither outside nor inside and needed to be protected against dangerous magic. And in one of Aunt Mary's books, it talked about how in traditional England you had to put a charm in your chimney to keep the smoke going out and stop spirits from coming in."

"Did this look like a northern beach? One here?"

"It was dark, so I couldn't really see. The woman had an Orcadian accent, though. I've heard it in the pub and from our landlady. It's very different than the usual Scottish accent."

"Some islanders don't consider themselves Scots

at all. Did Montague appear in the other two dreams?"

"No, and I don't think he was a part of them. I don't think he sent them my way. You know how sometimes you'll dream of something and associate the dream with someone even though they're not in it? I didn't get that."

"Interesting. And that dream in which he appears, I don't think that was a conscious move on Montague's part at all. He seems stuck, somehow."

"We need to help him."

Lucas shrugged. "We need to find out what's wrong with him first." Reluctantly he stood. "We should tell the others."

Della gave a crooked smile. "Yeah, before Sebastian comes back. I wanted to run it by you first."

That made him feel good, yet he felt compelled to ask, "Why? I'm the least knowledgeable person here except for Sebastian."

"That's why. It's easier with you. Sure, Richard can tell me more, and so can Cassandra, but they're so beyond me with this stuff it's a bit intimidating."

"Intimidating? I've never heard anyone call either of them intimidating."

"Maybe that's not the right word. They know so much more than me about this that I feel like I'm trying to talk about higher mathematics with some Oxford physicist."

Ah, Della. So that's it. You were so comfortable in your little academic bubble where you were the most knowledgeable person around, and now you're in the big, bad world. Lucas checked himself. *Well, I suppose I've been doing the same thing with my country walks and woodworking. And now we're both in a place we've never been fighting a force we don't understand. So I guess the best thing is to get back to it.*

"No need to feel out of sorts with Richard. He likes you and understands the whole 'reluctant practitioner' thing. He's friends with me, after all. And he's friends with you too. He loves you to pieces." That brought a smile to Della's lips. "As for Cassandra..." The smile vanished. "She's rather difficult, I agree. But we need her. She's every bit as powerful as Richard. Yes, she can be rather snippy. You just need to remember that she's on our side."

Della gave a little shrug and nodded. "She risked her life down in London for something that had nothing to do with her."

"Yes, she did. And now she's risking her life again. Let's go talk with them."

Lucas reached his arm around Della's shoulders

to give her a hug, hesitated just before making contact, and ended up giving her a little pat on the back.

A few minutes later in the common room, Richard and Cassandra mulled over what Della had revealed.

"Lucas is right about the Montague dream," Cassandra said. "He's radiating information without really being conscious he's doing it. He addressed you directly before, but in this instance, his spirit is perhaps anxious about something, and that's what Della picked up."

"If he's anxious, why hasn't he tried to get in direct contact?" Della asked.

"Who knows?" Richard said, throwing up his hands in frustration. "We need to try and contact him, and we need to get some more insight into what's going on here. Della, how long do you think your ex is going to be drinking with Bjorn the Viking?"

"No idea. Sebastian texted me half an hour ago to say they were done with the emergency services at Maeshowe, so if they only stay for one pint, they should be finishing up pretty soon."

"Bjorn doesn't strike me as a one-pint sort of chap," Lucas said.

"I agree," Richard said. "I think we should risk it. The only other option is to sneak out at night and do it in some field, but he's sure to hear us leave. Cassandra, help me prepare."

Lucas went over to the front door of the rental flat, hoping there was a chain or a bolt so they could keep Sebastian out if he returned early. He cursed under his breath when he didn't find one. Orkney probably had a low crime rate and such extra precautions weren't considered necessary.

Having cleared the living room of furniture, Richard and Cassandra laid out the tarp they had used in the previous ritual back in London. Once again, Richard set out a candle, lit it while muttering an invocation, and encircled it with ritually prepared powder. Della went around shutting all the blinds. Even though it was night and they didn't have to worry about daylight disrupting the invocation of any spirits, they certainly didn't want anyone spotting what they were doing from the windows across the street.

Lucas switched the lights off and went to stand on the tarp with the others. Cassandra drew a circle around them, and they stood together, eyes shut and opening their minds to any spiritual contacts.

Unlike the ritual in London, this time it did not take long.

Almost immediately after Richard and Cassandra finished the invocation and Lucas closed his eyes and opened his mind to the unseen world, he began to get a faint glimmer of contact.

It was Montague. Lucas did not see or hear him but sensed that his spirit was near.

Richard must have, too, because he heard his voice intone, "Montague, I ask you to make yourself known to the circle."

"Circle? What circle? Where?"

Montague's voice sounded a million miles away and yet could be heard clearly to all.

"Montague," Cassandra said, "follow the sound of my voice. You are lost. We need to help you find your way."

"Lost? Yes. I'm lost."

Montague's image slowly came into view behind Lucas's eyelids. The bookdealer stood against a background of darkness, moving this way and that and looking in all directions as if trapped in a labyrinth.

"It makes no sense," Montague said. "I shouldn't be here."

"Where should you be?" Lucas asked.

"I'm being held," Montague said. "They didn't

let me go to the other side, but they can't make me talk. I was prepared enough for that, at least."

"Who's holding you?" Della asked. "Who's trying to make you talk? About what?"

Montague shook his head. "They can't make me talk. I'm too strong for them but too weak to get to the other side."

He's not fully engaged with us, Lucas thought. *The connection isn't clear. That's probably the work of whoever is holding him between worlds.*

"We'll get you to the other side," Cassandra said. "But you need to tell us what's going on."

Montague's head jerked down, and he looked at something Lucas could not see, something below his feet, although his feet stood on nothing but darkness.

"They're coming," he said and winked out of sight.

For a moment, all was silent.

"I think—" Della began.

Cassandra shushed her.

They waited. Lucas could feel something move, some hidden power shift.

Montague reappeared. He looked down and to his left, eyes going wide. He waved a hand, as if telling them to go away, and then winked out of sight.

But the darkness all around him did not remain darkness. Slowly, a group of faces began to emerge from the background. Baleful eyes gazed at them from beneath red woolen caps. Their skin was greenish gray, and their expressions showed pure hatred.

They've found us, Lucas thought, his heart clenching.

"What the hell is going on here?"

Sebastian's voice cut through the vision. He flicked on the light, and the vision vanished, the connection with the other world severed.

Lucas opened his eyes. Sebastian stood, jaw hanging, in the doorway. His hand was still on the light switch.

"Well you sure have a hell of a sense of timing," Lucas growled.

"What's going on?" Della's ex demanded a second time. "I go for a pint and come back to find you in some witchcraft ritual?"

Richard shrugged. "You should be grateful, darling. At least we weren't all naked."

The look on Sebastian's face made his unexpected arrival almost worth it.

I guess we should be grateful too, Lucas thought. *He just saved us from another spiritual battle.*

14

DCI MATTHEWS FELT like a prospector who had just struck a vein of gold. Sebastian Davies had found evidence that those three were back up to their old tricks and, even better, were probably planning a break-in on public property.

Of course, Mr. Camilo and Mr. Lancaster had both been brought up on similar charges before. They had also resisted questioning in such circumstances. One of the frustrations of police work was that while you could arrest someone for something, you couldn't make them tell you why they had committed a crime. While most of the time the answer was obvious, it wasn't so with these two. But it was a start, and being far away from home and desperate to make contact with the Orkney occult circle, they were sure to slip up.

Mr. Davies had called shortly after seven in the evening, babbling about burning burial mounds and witchcraft rituals in the living room of their Airbnb. It took the police officer some time to calm the man down, and only then did he get a coherent story out of him.

So it looked like these clowns didn't know the occult group up in Orkney. Instead, they were opposed to them. Good. That meant a fight, and *that* meant felony convictions for all of them. His job now was to make sure their homicides were only attempted homicides.

DCI Matthews sat alone in his office. Most of the staff had left. Only the night shift was downstairs taking care of the drunks and the brawlers. The regular police could handle that sort of thing. He was more interested in what was going on in Orkney.

He had to get up there.

But how? He leaned back in his chair and looked past his computer at the wanted posters and charts of crime statistics, as if they could provide an answer. He couldn't exactly tell his chief that he wanted to fly to the other end of the British Isles to break up a fight between two groups of satanists or pagans or whatever the hell they were. The old man would never agree to that on expenses. And he couldn't go up there on his own hook. That was against regulations.

Unless he could build a case against them right away...

He pulled up the incident reports Richard Camilo had made with the London police. A friend on the force down there had tipped him off about them. Mr. Camilo had reported two separate burglary attempts on the premises of Mr. Summers, whose estate he was taking care of. Mr. Camilo had been able to ID both suspects via CCTV footage, and when faced with police, both suspects had pled guilty. They were members of London's occult community but from all reports were neither well connected nor well liked. They were also amateurs when it came to crime. Real bunglers. Both were first-time offenders, so DCI Matthews doubted they'd get much of a punishment. He couldn't put much leverage on them, and it didn't appear that they knew much anyway.

So what sent Mr. Camilo and his friends up to Orkney all of a sudden? Mr. Davies said there was some rival occult group up there that was after Mr. Summers's books but didn't know much in the way of detail. He wasn't the greatest of informants, that was for sure.

DCI Matthews got on the national police database and looked for incident reports for the Orkney islands. He spent a good hour scrolling through reports of drunk driving, affray outside of pubs, the occasional domestic incident, and possession of controlled substances. My God, why did criminals have to be so mundane? He had to hand it to these occultists. At least they were original. Most criminals had the same list of drearily predictable offenses. Dull as dishwater, although arresting them still gave him a good feeling inside. Society had to punish people like that, and punish them properly.

"Oh, here's one," he said with a chuckle. "Suspected attempted break-in of the Kirkwall morgue. No charges filed due to lack of evidence. Meh. Just some teen prank. Points for originality, though."

Yes, just the routine crimes by the routine criminals. Far more serious was the hidden occult community, a community that the police were only dimly aware of. Every now and then there would be some big incident, like Mr. Lancaster's parents being abducted back in the nineties or the affair in Highgate Cemetery back in the seventies. And of course the events in Oxfordshire had made headlines. But the short attention span of the press had already moved on to other things, and the police force had done the same. It saw occult crimes as something unusual, generally unrelated to the regular background noise of substance abuse and petty violence.

DCI Matthews wasn't so sure. If these people were committing murder left and right, who knew what lesser crimes they got up to? Perhaps these occult circles operated like criminal gangs. He'd seen one of Mr. Summers's occult book catalogs. Some of the volumes cost three months' wages for a man like him. He had a copy on his desk. *The Wonders of the Invisible World* by someone named Cotton Mather went for £15,000. Granted, it had been printed in 1693 and covered the Salem witch trials from the point of view of an eyewitness, but it wasn't even a first edition. The catalog did have a first edition of *The Confessions of Aleister Crowley* that went for "only" £750, but the bloody thing had been published in 1969, so it was hardly a historical artifact. Besides, there were modern editions on Amazon for £35. You had to be either very rich or very stupid to pay prices like that, and those two categories, in DCI Matthews's experience, often went hand in hand.

So he had an idea that perhaps these occult

circles were made up of more than just rich recluses like Montague Summers and half-starved boffins on the fringe like those two idiots arrested for trying to break into his home. Perhaps the people in these occult organizations were running drugs or arms or stolen goods. Perhaps they were responsible for a fair bit of crime. No normal person would summon up demons or ghosts.

Ghosts...

DCI Matthews shuddered. The vision in the tunnels beneath King's Cross still haunted him.

He began to scroll through the recent crimes in Orkney again, looking at them with a fresh set of eyes. No shortage of illegal drugs in the far north. People probably got bored during the long winter nights. Such a rural place with a small population probably only had one gang running the show, plus a few individuals scoring pills or grass down in one of the bigger Sottish cities and sneaking it up there. Easy enough to do on the ferry. What if that one big gang was a group of occultists?

No way to tell from the records, though. He went back a good six months and didn't find anything out of order, nothing that hinted at a larger group behind these mundane crimes.

Then he did a wider search, and instantly came up with something interesting.

All he did was google "occultists in Orkney," and the first thing he came up with was an article in *The Orcadian Online* from four months before titled "Frederick MacHugh, Local Occultist and Recluse, Dies Age 87."

"Coincidence?" he said to himself. "I don't think so."

The article didn't tell him much, because on the surface there wasn't much to tell. Mr. MacHugh of the island of Stronsay had inherited a small fortune at a young age and had devoted his life to studying the hidden world. He had no close family, apparently no friends, and the reporter couldn't even get a quote from anyone. Recluse, indeed.

Then it hit him—the date.

He went back to the attempted break-in at the morgue. Yes, the dates matched, and Kirkwall's morgue was the only one on the islands. Had some occultist tried to break in to do something with Mr. MacHugh's corpse? He remembered reading somewhere that back in the witchcraft days, people would pull teeth from the mouths of hanged men to use them in spells. Maybe some local occultists wanted to do something similar.

He brought up the case file and began to read.

A patrol car spotted a man acting suspiciously near the city morgue at one o'clock in the morning, when it was dark even in an Orkney summer. Since the pubs had all closed two hours before and there was virtually no one on the streets, the officers noted him and circled around to take another look a couple of minutes later. He was still next to the morgue, just moving away from a window when the patrol car appeared on the street.

The police stopped him, and he gave some song and dance about waiting to see a girl he had met in a pub. The police didn't believe this story and believed it even less when they found the window to the morgue had been tampered with. Someone had been trying to work off the shutters with a pair of pliers, which were found behind a bush nearby. The suspect, whose name was James Firth, denied all knowledge but acted nervous and suspicious enough that they brought him in for further questioning.

He held up well under questioning, however, sticking to his story and saying he had no knowledge of the pliers or attempted break-in. He had no controlled substances on him, no prior convictions, and there were no prints on the pliers, so the police had no choice but to let him go. There was a note on the report to tell both shifts to keep an eye on the man.

DCI Matthews did a computer search for James Firth and found that he was a fisherman who lived on Stronsay, the same island as the deceased occultist. Considering that the island had a population of only 349 people, it was difficult to believe this was a coincidence. The officer's skepticism was further aroused when he discovered Firth had written several articles for occult magazines on something called "ley energy."

Whatever the hell that was.

DCI Matthews felt out of his depth. He had a feeling that if he got into a conversation with this fisherman about his hobby, he wouldn't understand a bloody word he said.

So Mr. Firth was a neighbor of a reclusive occultist and tried to do something with his body after he died. He scoured the police records again, and while he found no evidence of a break-in at the deceased occultist's house, he did find a request from the next of kin, who lived in Edinburgh, for the police to check on the house and oversee it being locked up and fitted with a burglar system. The reason given was that the house was full of valuable books and the family worried they might get stolen.

Given the prices DCI Matthews had seen in that catalog, he didn't blame them.

He found another note a month later saying that the burglar alarm was gone and the family had removed all valuable items from the house. The property was now up for sale.

Searching through *The Orcadian Online*, he found another reference to Frederick MacHugh from a month after he died. "Local Occultist's Library Auctioned Off." Details were vague, but the brief article mentioned that the most valuable volumes had been sold to "London's leading dealer in occult books."

That would be Montague Summers.

"Well, isn't this getting tied up in a tidy bow?"

DCI Matthews chewed his lip. Not tidy enough. He still didn't have enough evidence to nab anyone or get travel funds to go up there.

Sebastian Davies needed to give him something juicy.

Then the answer became obvious. It wasn't professionally ethical, it wasn't moral, it wasn't even legal, but it would get him what he needed.

It would involve him doing something he had never done before in his decades of service. It twisted his gut a bit knowing he was even considering it.

And yet it was the only choice he had. If he wanted to stop these people, if he wanted to avoid a bloodbath off the north coast of Scotland, he'd have to do it. He would swallow his scruples in order to stop a murder, or murders.

But would Sebastian Davies do it? Yes, he would, because he was a weak little toff, and DCI Matthews was an officer of the law who had him backed into a corner.

The officer winced. What he was doing was a foul thing, an utterly unprofessional thing. He soothed his conscience by telling himself the sad truth that it was a necessary thing.

Still, the word did not sit well with him.

Entrapment.

Planting the seeds on an online forum was a simple trick. He was savvy enough with computers to backdate a post and then add a short thread with several fake accounts. He was also savvy enough not to do this on his police computer, but with his own computer at home via the dark web.

Once finished, he called Sebastian Davies. He gave the young man explicit instructions about what to tell his friends and what he should get them to do.

After that, he called the Orkney police.

15

JUST AS DELLA suspected all along, Sebastian had not taken the ritual well. He had stared at them like he had come back to the apartment expecting to see a normal group of people and was instead greeted by a freak show.

For a moment, Della felt embarrassed. Here they were, four grown adults, standing in a circle of yellow powder with the lights off, communing with ghosts. From the outside, it looked absolutely ridiculous. It kind of looked ridiculous from her point of view too.

Except that it worked.

"What in the world are you doing?" he demanded.

"We *were* performing a ritual to speak with a dead friend until you interrupted," Richard said.

Della winced then shrugged. Now that he had caught them in the act, maybe it was time for the direct approach.

"That cult I told you about is trying to steal some valuable books from Montague's estate. We thought he might know more about it, so we got into contact."

"With your dead friend."

"Yes."

"You talked to your dead friend in order to get clues about an evil cult working in Scotland."

"Yes."

Sebastian shook his head and walked out.

"That went rather well," Richard said.

"Should I go after him?" Della asked.

"Let him process this for a bit," he said, beginning to clear up the ritual area. Cassandra helped.

Della stood there a minute, unsure what to do next.

"Maybe I should call him."

"He'll work through it himself and get back to us," Richard said. "He'll come around. It's hard to accept these things at first."

"It would help if he had felt anything at the ley

nexus," Lucas said, slumping on the couch. "I still don't understand why his power isn't manifesting."

"Neither do I," Richard said.

"I'm going to call him," Della said.

"Waste of time. Leave him be," Richard said.

She did anyway. His phone was busy.

Great, Della thought. *He's probably calling all our friends back in Oxford and telling them what a nutcase I am.*

She paused for a moment.

What friends? I've cloistered myself in the lab and library so much that I hardly have any friends. I can count my friends on one hand, and they're all here.

And I have a feeling I have one less now.

A few minutes later, Sebastian returned. He looked uncomfortable and didn't meet anyone's eye. An awkward silence filled the apartment. Della sat in a corner, pretending to use her phone while looking up enough to give Sebastian a chance to speak with her. Richard and Cassandra flicked on the television, and Lucas fiddled around in the kitchen for a bit until Sebastian cleared his throat.

"Look... I, um, I'm sorry I broke your ritual. I've been meaning to ask you something. Bjorn and I stayed at Maeshowe until the fire crew got finished.

They couldn't find anything wrong with the electrical system, no reason why it should have shorted out. I also noticed that all of you looked sick and unsteady there, and at the stone circles too. Della fell over. Was that witchcraft?"

"Imprecise term," Richard said, muting the television and turning to him. "It's ley energy."

"Ley lines. Yeah, I've heard of them. Never given them much thought. Look, I did a bit of research online before coming up here, trying to figure out what was going on since Della didn't see fit to tell me anything substantive. Did you know a famous occultist died here a few months back?"

"Yes," Della said. "That's one of the reasons we're up here."

"Ah, well, someone was caught trying to break into his house."

Richard perked up. "Really? But that house has been cleared out."

"So you do know about it," Sebastian said.

"About the occultist, not about the break-in. Where did you find this information? His next of kin didn't mention it."

"I'm not sure they knew. Here, let me find it."

Sebastian went to his room and pulled out his laptop, and everyone gathered around. Della was irritated to see that when Sebastian sat on the couch, Cassandra went behind him and leaned over, showing off her cleavage. Della got some pleasure from the fact that Sebastian didn't even notice. No one had seen fit to tell Cassandra that Sebastian was unavailable in a most fundamental way. She wondered if they all got the same devious pleasure from it that she did.

Sebastian got onto a small forum called "Northern Mysteries." Judging from the subject lines, it was devoted mostly to Wicca and alternative archaeology in Scotland. He scrolled down a long way before finding a thread titled "MacHugh House Ritual Break-in."

"I recognized the name from an obituary I found online," Sebastian explained. "When you said you had some occult group up here in Orkney, I did an internet search and found out about this fellow Frederick MacHugh on one of the smaller islands. He was an occultist who died a few months ago."

"Yes, that's the man whose estate my friend purchased," Richard said. "Now I'm stuck with the books, and someone is trying to get them."

"That's what I thought. So I did some background work and found this."

Richard smiled. "My, my, you've been a busy bee. Why didn't you tell us earlier?"

"I, um, didn't know if you'd take it seriously or if it was pertinent to the case. I, um, sorry…"

Della studied her ex-boyfriend. He was blushing, and his words came out haltingly. He still wouldn't look at any of them.

He must be embarrassed that he's finally taking all this seriously, Della assumed. *I sure know how that feels.*

Sebastian opened up the thread. It was dated from a month before and had only a few responses.

The thread started with a post saying that some user called witch666 had a dream that a great treasure was buried under the MacHugh house and that she had summoned her familiar to go search it out. "As you know," the poster wrote, "the famous MacHugh library had already been cleared out, which is why my dream felt so important. I became convinced that there was something there the estate sale missed. My familiar searched the house high and low and could not find it, although it sensed a great magical energy. We have to go there in person to find it. Who's with me?"

There followed an argument in which some posters said it was wrong to break into a dead man's house, another warned of a curse on the property, and another poster, named DarkArts, simply said, "DM me." The thread stopped at that point until a final post five days later from a new poster who gleefully wrote, "witch666 and DarkArts got busted trying to break into the MacHugh house! They're being arraigned in Kirkwall for burglary. Never liked those two. White magic is stronger than black!"

"They missed something," Della said. "The next of kin missed something, and the local group sensed it. That's why they tried to get into the house."

"Could be," Richard said. "From what I know, MacHugh's next of kin was not close to him, and none of them dabbled in the hidden arts. They would not have thought to search the house for hiding places, and MacHugh would not have told them."

Cassandra leaned a little closer to Sebastian's laptop, purportedly to read the thread again. "From what I heard, he was quite secretive. I doubt he told anyone any details of what he did in his house beyond what was absolutely necessary for performing group rituals. There might be all sorts of lovely goodies in there."

"This thread is strange, though," Richard said, frowning. "It's written in such an amateurish fashion, as if by a bunch of people who know nothing of true magic."

"Perhaps it's a code?" Lucas suggested.

"If so, it's not a very subtle one."

"Perhaps they are newbies," Della said. It seemed amateurish even to her amateurish eyes. "But this witch666 person has a bit of the Talent and really did sense something."

"This talk of a familiar is nonsense," Cassandra said. "They don't work the way this person says they work. And any practitioner powerful enough to actually have a familiar wouldn't be chatting on some cheap online forum."

"So she's lying about that," Della said with a shrug. "There are plenty of people in the occult community who exaggerate their abilities or pretend to knowledge they don't have. I think we should check it out."

Sebastian hung his head, looking dejected.

Della looked at him with sympathy. *You're really having a hard time with this, aren't you? But it's all beginning to sink in.*

"I agree," Lucas said. "While Maeshowe is obviously a center of the disturbance, we're going to have a tough time getting back in there after what happened, and we still don't know exactly what's going on. Perhaps we can find out what's souring the ley lines."

Richard rubbed his chin. "MacHugh could have left some powerful ritual unfinished when he died. That might have done it."

Cassandra flicked her long hair. "Perhaps you've been getting all this wrong. If this local group wants the books to fix the problem, maybe they aren't the enemy."

"If they weren't the enemy," Della said with deliberation, "then they wouldn't have had the fire spirit attack us. They would have approached us openly."

"Besides, the books only protect you from problems with the ley lines. They don't fix them," Richard said.

Sebastian threw his hands in the air. "I have absolutely no idea what you people are nattering on about!"

Richard patted his thigh. "You just sit there and look pretty."

"We should go to his house and take a look around," Della said. "That person who started the forum chat actually gives the GPS coordinates. Good way to telegraph that you're about to commit a crime. No wonder they got caught. If we're more careful than they are, perhaps we can find traces of the ritual and that will give us a clue."

Sebastian started tapping away on his laptop.

"What are you doing?" Della asked.

"Instead of looking pretty," Sebastian grumbled, "I'm looking up ferries from Mainland to Stronsay. Looks like there are two round trips a day, one in the morning and one in the afternoon. The ferry takes nearly two hours."

"Then we should get the morning one," Della said. "Are there hotels there, just in case we don't get everything done before the evening ferry leaves?"

Sebastian did a bit more searching. "There are a couple of guest houses, both shut because it's off season."

"Let's risk it," Della said.

So the next morning, when the sun had not yet risen on the rainy northern winter's day, they bundled into a ferry at Kirkwall harbor. The ferry was a wide, hulking steel ship with room for cars to drive onto the back. Only a few did, and the spartan seating area inside with its steel floors and hard plastic seats was all but empty. Only a few other people, obviously locals, sat reading or looking absently out the rain-streaked windows at the lights of the harbor. It was cold, and the seas looked rough. Della wondered if Cassandra would get sick again.

With a sound of the horn, the ferry began to pull out. It passed the harbor's few piers where fishing boats with bright-red hulls and white cabins bobbed in the water. Sebastian went to the far end of the sitting area and started texting. Della put up the hood of her raincoat and went outside to get a better look.

Sharp sea air filled her lungs. Out on the water, it felt colder, and a soft rain fell, making the deck slick and spraying her face as it came down at an angle thanks to the strong breeze. All this was outweighed by the sweeping view.

The sun peeked over the eastern horizon. The clouds did not reach it, and in the distance, the sea shimmered gold.

Kirkwall rested in a wide bay. The town fronted the harbor, dominated by a large brick hotel of the Victorian era. Bjorn said they served good meals. He had made it sound like an invitation. After the craziness of the previous day, however, she wasn't sure that invitation still stood. He hadn't called, and he hadn't been asked to come along on this trip. Della felt a mixture of disappointment and relief. Things were coming to a head, and it would be best if an innocent like Bjorn stayed well clear.

He'd been nice, though, intelligent and interesting.

And completely unavailable, Della told herself. *He lives hundreds of miles away from you.*

Those thoughts passed as she surveyed the view around her. The ferry was pulling away from the harbor now, the red-and-white fishing boats and the redbrick town dwindling, more of her view taken up with the waters of the bay turned golden by the rising sun. Ahead, right in the middle of the bay, she saw a little skerry, barely twenty yards across, tufted with grass and dotted with cawing seagulls.

The prison for Norsemen, she remembered. *The one Sebastian told us about.*

She opened her mind up to the ambient energies, wondering if she would feel something off of it, but they passed it too far and too quickly.

Perhaps if I actually went and stood on it, I'd feel something.

Della filled her lungs with sea air and smiled. As terrifying and confusing as this newfound ability could be, it was also fascinating. She'd learned of a whole new way to look at the world. She asked herself, if given the choice between living as she was now or going back to her more innocent and ignorant self, what she would choose. To her mild surprise, she realized that she would not go back to the way things were before. She had grown, and as painful as that growth was, it was necessary. And what she was doing now was important.

If Richard's interpretation of the Orcadian magic proved correct, the ley lines could affect the whole world. She was safer facing this thing head-on than staying clueless and attending her lectures back in Oxford. Some things affected everyone, and ignorance did not save you.

The ferry let out a long call with its horn. Three horns responded. Della turned from where she had been watching the receding town and leaned over the railing to look toward where the bay let out onto the open ocean. Three fishing boats were entering in a line, coming back from the night's catch. One by one they passed, giving out another call with their horns, the captains at the helm waving to the captain of the ferry.

The sea got choppier as they passed from the protection of the harbor into open water. Della moved from the stern past the few cars and along the edge of the main cabin to the prow, gripping the handrail as the water got rougher. Once she got to the prow, she planted her feet well apart and held the handrail in front of her with both hands. Above and behind her, she could see the captain at the wheel behind the window. He was the only person she could see. For a moment, she felt embarrassed. He probably thought she was some tourist doing an imitation of that silly *Titanic* movie. Then she realized he wasn't paying attention to her at all. He had a more important job to do.

So did Della. She realized she probably should be back in the cabin planning strategy with the others, but the pull of the open sea was too strong. She needed to get away from them for a while, and this beautiful view was the best place to do so.

They left the harbor behind, and the North Sea opened up before her. While to the right and left and ahead she could see other islands, low stretches of grass or rockier eminences, most of her view was taken up by open sea.

The wind blew spray in her face, and the sea grew rougher, rolling the ship up swells and down troughs. She didn't feel afraid, though. She noticed the railing was set well back from the actual edge of the prow, no doubt to keep people like her from taking an accidental plunge.

While the winds remained strong and the seas

rough, the sky above cleared, and they now sailed through full sunlight. Cassandra joined her at the prow.

Of all people to interrupt my solitude. Couldn't she puke somewhere else?

Della was surprised to notice that she didn't look sick, as she had on the plane.

"You feeling all right?" Della asked.

"Oh, lovely." She certainly looked chipper.

"I figured you'd be sick in this weather. I'm surprised I'm not."

"I don't get seasick, darling. I've been on far rougher seas than this and felt fine. I'm attuned to water magic."

"Oh." Della felt a guilty sense of disappointment. "I've heard a lot of practitioners are attuned to a certain type of magic. Why did you decide to work on water magic?"

If she was going to be stuck with Cassandra on deck, she might as well learn something.

"I didn't choose water magic. It chose me. Those with the Talent are attuned to different flavors of magic and find their way to them if they open themselves up to being led. Lucas is attuned to ley and nature magic, although he isn't really attuned to anything because he insists on not studying. Try as I might, I could not get that lovely man to put in the work. Dear old Richard is more of a ceremonial magic type of practitioner. He has earned a great deal of respect in occult circles for fusing different traditions and creating more powerful rituals than any one tradition could on its own."

"So, do I have some type of magic I'm attuned to?"

"I'm sure you do. Keep studying it and you'll find it."

Della looked out at the approaching island. "It seems everything that happens to me is related to the ley lines. Maybe that's what I'm attuned to."

"Perhaps."

"Or maybe ancient sites? Maybe that's why I became an archaeologist in the first place. My subconscious was leading me in the right direction."

"I don't think so, darling. Ancient sites aren't magic in themselves. They become magic because they are sacred sites put along ley lines. You have a lot to learn about real archaeology."

Della seethed. It was bad enough that this woman constantly condescended to her. She was not about to stand being lectured about archaeology by someone who had never studied the subject.

Cassandra gave her a sympathetic look. "If you

are attuned to ley lines, you've picked a bad time to discover your Talent. You should have learned of it years ago. We're going to need both you and Lucas for whatever it is we're facing. Richard and I can't do it alone. What worries me most, though, is that neither of you are ready. Knowing a little about magic is far, far more dangerous than knowing nothing about magic at all."

16

THE TRIP HAD LEFT Lucas feeling invigorated. The cluster of ley lines crisscrossing the islands did not reach up this far north, and indeed he had seen on the government maps he'd brought along that there were few archaeological sites on Stronsay. He felt surprised that an occultist like MacHugh would want to avoid such things. He could have lived on Mainland and been at the epicenter of one of the most powerful ley nexuses on the planet.

Maybe that's why he lived here, to get away from all that. Man after my own heart.

As the ferry pulled into Whitehall harbor and docked at the port's lone pier, Lucas saw just how much that was true. The town couldn't have had more than fifty buildings, all uniformly low and gray, as if hugging the ground for fear of being blown away by the rough northern winds. The map said it was the biggest settlement on the whole island.

One car pulled off the back of the ferry, the driver giving them a curious glance before heading across the pier and disappearing into town. They got off, stopped by a pile of fish boxes and heaps of green netting, and studied the map. The forum post Sebastian had found had given the address and GPS coordinates of MacHugh's house. It was a good five kilometers away, and Lucas didn't think there was much public transport on this island.

The ferry sounded its horn and pulled away, headed for even more remote islands before looping back to Kirkwall. Suddenly Lucas felt very isolated.

"This road looks like the quickest way to make it there," he said, tracing it with his finger.

Richard glanced at the nearest buildings—a harbormaster's shed and a community shop. Curtains twitched in the windows of both buildings.

"That might look a bit conspicuous," he said. He pointed to the shoreline. "Why don't we go along the beach this way and then cut overland? It won't be much farther, and we'll look more like tourists."

Lucas smiled as his friend. "Are you saying we stand out here?"

"A Yank, a fashionable London girl, a Home Counties farmer, and dashing young man new to the gay scene? Who would think?" Richard glanced at the buildings again then cupped his hand and said in a dramatic whisper, "Besides, I might be the first black person they've ever seen. We don't want to startle the natives."

"Beach it is, then," Cassandra said with a smile.

"Perhaps you can cast a spell to keep the rain away," Lucas said. Although the sky had cleared above them, he saw a foreboding line of gray clouds on the horizon.

Sebastian laughed then looked at them curiously.

One step at a time, newbie, Lucas thought. He still didn't want the chap here. He had been proving useful, though. And even after being startled by the sight of them all within a summoning circle, he had come around quickly enough. Surprisingly quickly.

It took all of three minutes to get out of town. Beyond lay open green fields, shining bright in the sun. The island was mostly flat, and they could see far.

There wasn't much to see, only open space, the occasional stout stone farmhouse, a few flocks of sheep, and seagulls wheeling high above.

A trail past the last house led through tall grass to

the beach, which was surprisingly beautiful—broad and clean with pale sand and not a building in sight. Anywhere else, it would have been crowded with tourists and lined with resort hotels. Here, though, they had to bundle up in sweaters and raincoats, and instead of enjoying the feel of sand between their toes, they clomped along in heavy, waterproof boots. They walked quickly, knowing they only had a few hours to get their work done.

"Fantastic," Cassandra whispered.

"I figured you'd prefer the Costa del Sol or the south of France," Della said.

Cassandra shook her head. "I do like my nightlife, but not on my beaches. I want them clean, pristine."

"Like Thames Water," Richard said and chuckled.

"One does what one can," Cassandra replied with a smile.

They walked in silence for a time, enjoying the quiet and openness of this remote island. Lucas noted an incredible variety of birds—not just the ubiquitous seagulls, but also Arctic terns with their white bodies topped by black feathers like caps on their heads and thin red beaks; great skuas with their brown-and-tan speckled feathers and their puffed out chests making them look like they were about to give an important speech; and a flock of redshanks that ran back and forth with each lapping wave, hunting for sea creatures, their brown-and-white-speckled bodies carried on the skinny red legs that gave them their name.

Far up ahead, they saw a large gray form in the sand.

"What's that?" Richard asked.

"Perhaps it's the Stronsay Beast," Cassandra said.

"Please don't tell me we have to contend with cryptids as well," Richard said.

"What's a cryptid?" Della asked.

"An animal unidentified by science," Sebastian said. When Richard turned to him with surprise, he shrugged and said, "You learn a lot channel surfing late at night. I've never heard of the Stronsay Beast, though."

Cassandra brushed a stray lock of hair out of her eyes and said, "It was a strange sea creature that washed up on the beach here two hundred years ago. A huge thing, more than fifty feet long, and part of it was missing, so it might have been much bigger. It was gray, with a fat body, fins, and a long, thin neck. The people who saw it dubbed it a sea serpent, although more modern investigators think it might have been a plesiosaur like the Loch Ness Monster. Of course, it was no such thing."

"Oh, a globster!" Sebastian said. "I've heard of those. They've been found all over. There was one in the Philippines a few year ago. Probably decomposed basking sharks. I don't think that's a globster up ahead, though. It looks more like a seal."

Cassandra looked at him. "Sebastian, you are a towering genius."

Glad I'm not the only one who's sick of him, Lucas thought. *But she's just mad because he won't respond to her passes. And that's turned her more on me again. Bloody hell, I'd probably have to pair up with Sebastian to get her to leave me alone.*

They approached the seal, which looked at them askance with its liquid black eyes before flopping its way into the surf.

Lucas stopped and studied the map. "Looks like once we pass that little bay we're coming to, there's a trail inland that will take us to MacHugh's house."

"Just in time for that storm to dump on us," Della said.

The line of clouds had approached quickly. While it didn't look like a proper storm, the gray wall between the clouds and the sea heralded a good soaking rain.

"The weather changes every ten minutes in this place," Lucas said.

"Unless it's rain," Sebastian said. "Then it can last for days. Bjorn told me that last winter—"

"I'm not interested in what Bjorn says," Lucas snapped.

The others looked at him, but he didn't bother to look back. He didn't want to be here. He wanted to be back on the farm taking care of the flock and making his furniture, not on some remote beach with two people he didn't want to spend time with and about to be rained on while headed for what would surely be a dangerous situation in some dead occultist's house.

The rain came right on schedule, a steady, slanting downpour that made them turn their faces from the stiff breeze blowing in off the sea. That did not help Lucas's mood.

They found the trail past a few more beached seals and headed inland, grateful to have their backs to the driving rain. They'd been walking for the better part of an hour, and they hadn't seen a soul. Lucas wondered how they would get help if one of them got hurt. He wasn't sure there was even mobile coverage here. He decided not to check. He'd lost his last mobile phone to the rain when his discount daypack turned out not to be as waterproof as the label claimed.

The path led them over the humps of a couple of dunes and then straight between two open fields. As they trudged along, Lucas opened up his mind to any ambient magical energies and found none. Aunt Mary's map was right. There were no ley lines running through here.

Precious little of anything else either. He counted a grand total of three farmhouses within view, none of them close, and a single car traveling along a distant road. When they passed over a low hill and came down the other side, even those scant signs of civilization vanished.

Before them spread a gentle slope leading down to the eastern coast of the island. Instead of a beach, the land cut off on a rugged cliff. The path took them along the top of it. The rain slackened but showed no signs of stopping.

"Careful on this bit," Lucas said. On their right-hand side, there was nothing but a steep slope of slick grass before a sheer drop to surf-lashed rocks.

They went single file for another kilometer before stopping. Before them was a narrow inlet where the sea had gouged out a portion of the cliff as if slicing a piece off with a knife. A natural rock bridge spanned the distance, and the path ran right over it. The water that had cut the inlet had started by boring out a tunnel, and years of weathering had taken off all of the tunnel's roof except for a span of thick stone several meters wide.

According to the map, MacHugh's house was just over the hill they could see beyond the natural bridge, but the idea of crossing that bridge filled him with foreboding.

"Maybe we should go around," Della said in a soft voice.

"I feel it too," Richard said.

Cassandra nodded.

"What?" Sebastian asked with a shrug. "The path looks wide enough."

It's not the path we're worried about.

Lucas studied the map. If they wanted to go around, they would have to retrace their steps all the way to town and take the road. Given the short winter days, that would leave them with very little time at the house before they had to return to the ferry. They could cut over the fields and go around the inlet, but the way was muddy and slick and in two places blocked by barbed wire fences, no doubt to keep sheep from falling off the cliff in stormy weather. It was doable but would also waste time they didn't have.

It was probably best to do that anyway.

Just as he was about to suggest it, he found that his decision had already been made for him.

"Come on, everyone," Sebastian said, walking quickly ahead and getting on the natural bridge. "Do you want to get there or not? This rain isn't about to stop, and I wouldn't mind a hot cup of tea back in that village before taking the—"

He lurched to the side as if slammed by an invisible automobile, struck with sufficient force to be taken off his feet. He landed a meter to his right, skidding on the grass to one side of the path.

Skidding right for the edge.

Lucas ran for him, a sickening sensation clenching the pit of his stomach with the realization that he'd never make it in time. Sebastian's hands scrabbled for a grip on the wet grass, his body still sliding for the precipice, until his hands grasped a projecting stone.

The top of his body stopped, but he swung down the slope like a pendulum until his legs dangled over the edge. The jolt of that wasn't enough to jar his grip loose, but Lucas could see him weaken.

Eyes bulging, Sebastian pulled on the rock, dragging his body up the slope enough to get an unsteady foothold. Lucas was almost there, just a few more steps to the stone bridge. If Sebastian could just hold on for another few seconds, he could save him.

Lucas felt someone grab him by the waist and yank on him. He was pulled to a stop. A glance over his shoulder revealed that none of his friends had grabbed him. Indeed, all of them had been stopped too. Cassandra seemed to be struggling with an unseen opponent. Richard was down on one knee, trying to pull something from his pocket. Della struggled not far off, looking down at something Lucas could not see, terror in her eyes.

Lucas summoned up his willpower and tried to move forward. The grip on his waist lessened but did not free him.

Then, with startling clarity, he saw Sebastian's fingers get pried off the rock one by one by some invisible force.

Lucas was almost to him. The grip around his waist tightened, making him struggle. With a spike of fear, he realized that pull could turn into a push, sending him hurtling over the edge.

One of Sebastian's hands was jerked free. He immediately tried to grab the rock again, but his arm waved in the air, struggling against something. Then, one by one, the fingers of his remaining hand were peeled from the rock.

With sheer force of mental will, Lucas managed to wrench free of the otherworldly grip. The force of doing so made him tumble forward, his knees smacking painfully against the ground. His arms cartwheeled as he tried to get his balance on the slope, and then he fell to his stomach. For a heart-stopping second, he skidded for the edge before the rough ground halted him.

Someone was shouting in the background, but he couldn't focus on that now. Right in front of him, Sebastian was losing his final grip on safety.

Lucas shot his hands forward and grasped Sebastian's wrist just as the man's last finger was pried free. The instant he did so, he realized that Sebastian's weight would simply drag him over the edge too.

His heart skipped a beat, and for an unworthy second, he considered letting Sebastian go, but something inside him would not let him. He felt his body edge forward a few precious inches...

...and stop.

Sebastian had laid himself out flat on the slope as well to increase the friction of his body and slow his slide to oblivion. His hand and feet had managed to find enough purchase to stop their descent.

But he could not let go, and Lucas could not let go.

They were stuck there, poised on the edge.

Sebastian looked into his eyes. "Let me go."

"No."

Lucas sucked in a startled breath as he felt a pair of hands grasp the back of his shirt.

He clenched his eyes shut. He did not want to see Sebastian's face when the spirits pushed the both of them over the edge.

17

DELLA GRABBED at Lucas's coat and hauled him back from the edge with all her might. Years of archaeological excavations had made her strong, but Lucas weighed more than she did, and he was holding on to Sebastian. She planted her legs in a wide fencer's stance, hoping the unseen attacker she had managed to shove away wouldn't renew its attack.

She managed to pull Lucas back a few inches. Something pushed her at the small of her back, but her stance kept her from falling over.

She did have to stop pulling for a second. The two men were still helplessly stuck far too close to the edge. Della felt something grasp the front of her coat and looked with startled amazement as her coat pulled forward in two spots. She could even see the imprint of fingers.

Cassandra's and Richard's voices shouted out something in unison. Della caught a fragment of Medieval Latin, something about opening the path. She was a little too preoccupied at the moment to decipher dead languages.

The invisible fingers on her raincoat let go, the material falling back against her chest. Della grabbed Lucas by the belt with one hand and the collar with the other and gave another long pull.

Half lifting him, she dragged him back several feet, the two men still gripping each other's wrists, Sebastian helping by scrabbling with his feet until they were safely away from the slope.

The two men let go of each other and scrambled farther away from the rock bridge. Della followed, only to be stopped short by an invisible blow to her gut.

She doubled over, coughing and clutching her middle.

A strong hand gripped her wrist and spun her around to face the natural bridge. She saw a flicker of shadows in front of her, one of which was connected to her wrist. Della planted her feet and willed the shadows away.

No use. Her arm got wrenched so hard it felt like it might come out of its socket, and she stumbled forward.

Straight for the edge.

"No!" she shouted.

The beings flickered into view. Della screamed.

They were the same squat figures in rough homespun and red caps that she had seen in her dream and in her vision in the car coming from the airport.

Trolls.

But these were no longer dreams, no longer visions. Grinning with glee, they danced and capered as the one that had her by the wrist hauled her with unnatural strength toward her death.

Della leaned backward, playing tug of war with her own arm. The thing holding her gave her a hateful glare and pulled harder. Her boots skidded on the wet ground as, inch by inch, it pulled her to the edge.

She was not going to win this fight. Time for a change of tactics.

Summoning her will, she swung her free arm at the troll, fist clenched.

The thing winked out of view, as did all the others.

And Della realized she had fallen for a trick.

Because the motion of punching combined with suddenly being let go made her stumble forward, her body tipping, her feet slipping, and she knew she was going to go over.

Until she got pulled back at the last instant.

Sebastian.

Before he could lead her more than two steps to safety, the trolls reappeared in a ring all around them. Lucas was on the ground struggling with several more of them. Cassandra and Richard stood nearby chanting in Latin but could hardly be seen. It was as if a curtain of gauze had been lowered between them. Their images were hard to discern, their voices all but muted. Della sensed that whatever spell they were trying to cast, it would not work —or at least not work in time.

They were alone.

The trolls moved in.

"Go away!" Sebastian screamed, lashing out against the nearest one.

Della did not expect what happened next.

Sebastian hit the thing square on the jaw. There was a loud crack, and blood spouted from its mouth as it spun and fell.

Her ex turned and struck another one in the face,

sending it toppling backward. He swung at a third one, but only met air.

They had all vanished. The dark gauze had lifted.

That was the only incentive they needed to run full speed away from the natural bridge.

The others joined them without a word, and they hurried down the slope to where the path ran between two broad fields. No cliffs, no slope leading to oblivion. Safety.

Sebastian collapsed, falling into a seated position facing back the way they had come, eyes searching for invisible attackers. Della and the others stopped. Her lungs burned, and her stomach and wrist were still sore from where the trolls had attacked her.

Sebastian sat panting on the ground, his face shining with damp. Della figured that it was more sweat than rain.

"What the hell was that?" he demanded.

"Proof that all this is real," she said.

Sebastian swore, wiped his brow, and looked at the ground. A moment later, he looked around at each of them, perhaps hoping someone would contradict her.

"To be more precise," Cassandra said, "those were guardian spirits set up to bar our way."

"Spirits?" Sebastian almost shrieked.

"Like the ones you fought in my apartment," Della said. "And you fought them again here."

Her ex shook his head. "I... don't know how I did that."

Richard crouched next to him. "I'm not sure either. It appears you have a considerable affinity for magic, but it only comes out when you are in mortal danger."

He helped Sebastian up.

"Well don't put me in any more mortal danger!"

"I'm afraid it's too late for that," Richard said, patting him on the shoulder. "We have to forge ahead. It was your idea to come here in the first place."

"No, it wasn't. It was... I mean, yes."

Della looked at him curiously. "What do you mean?"

"Nothing. I'm all shook up. Ignore me. In fact, leave me alone and let me go back to Oxford." He turned toward the path to town.

"Sorry, we need you," Richard said. He hooked an arm through his. "Come on."

"We're not going back there!"

"The spirits are gone," Cassandra said. "You banished them. The path is safe now."

"You must be joking," Sebastian said.

"I felt them move back to their plane of existence," Richard said.

Della wasn't convinced either. "Are you sure?"

Richard put a hand on his shoulder. "Look, Sebastian. You need to gain confidence in your power. Now that you've seen the reality in which you live, the *real* reality, you need to understand it. There's nothing more dangerous to be than someone attuned to the hidden world who doesn't know what he's doing. I've seen a lot of people go mad or get killed doing that. It even happens to experienced occultists who get in over their heads."

Della remembered Cassandra's warning on the ferry and trembled.

"I don't want this," Sebastian said, trying to pull away.

"I know you don't. But it's real, and it's part of your life now. We don't have time to explain everything to you, just that we need to get to that house and discover what's going on or everyone, and I do mean everyone, might die. And no amount of willful ignorance will save you."

Sebastian looked at Della, perhaps hoping that she, who had always been so practical and rooted in the regular world, would contradict Richard. Instead, she only nodded grimly.

"Look," Richard said. "You stand back, and I'll walk across the rock bridge first. That way you'll see it's safe."

Sebastian did not look convinced. He did, however, allow himself to be led back up the slope to within view of the spot where they had been attacked.

Letting go of Sebastian, Richard began to step forward. Della joined him.

"Nice of you to volunteer," Richard said with a smile.

"Nobody else did," Della said in a low voice.

"Lucas can't sense the spirits are gone, and Cassandra is holding back, hoping to be the reassuring woman who will finally get Sebastian interested."

"You haven't told her about his orientation."

"Where's the fun in that? Neither have you, I see."

Della chuckled. Her friend had a knack for making tough situations feel easier.

But a bit of banter couldn't keep her heart from pounding as they approached the rock bridge. Her eyes darted in every direction, as if she could see the unseen things that might still lurk there.

"Did you see them?" she asked.

"Vaguely. The important thing is I don't sense them now."

Neither did Della, although she still didn't trust her instincts when it came to this stuff. It was like being asked to race in the Indy 500 right after getting her learner's permit.

"They looked like trolls from some folklore book."

"*Genius loci*, taking on the appearance that your mind has projected onto them. It's the reason people in the Middle Ages saw angels and nowadays we see aliens."

"I'd take an alien over one of those things."

"Careful. They might probe you."

"Shut up."

Richard's banter got them all the way to the natural bridge, at which point Della slowed, her guts growing cold. She pulled back her sleeve and saw her wrist was beginning to bruise.

"Steady," Richard said.

They stepped out on the bridge. In any other situation, it would be beautiful—a stony arch over a deep gorge with foaming waves, seagulls cawing overhead, the sea stretching out to one side with a flash of sunlight breaking through distant clouds. To Della, it only looked like a trap.

They stepped onto it. Della's senses were as sharp as a razor's edge. The muted colors of the rainy landscape looked clear and bright. The surf and bird-calls sounded overly loud. Even the smell of the sea was strong in her nostrils.

And yet she felt nothing beyond the ordinary.

They walked in silence. The rock bridge was only twenty meters or so long, and before they knew it, they were across.

Richard sighed. "I need a drink." He turned and motioned the others over. Lucas came next. Cassandra put a hand on Sebastian's arm, but he shrugged her off, motioned for her to wait, and walked over alone.

"Good boy," Richard said under his breath.

Cassandra came last, looking not entirely reassured that the others had made it over safely.

Once they were all gathered at a safe distance from the bridge, they took a breather. The rain continued unabated, but foul weather was the last thing on their minds.

"So why did those things attack us?" Sebastian asked.

"Perhaps they were guarding the natural bridge," Lucas said.

Sebastian shook his head. "The bridge was on the tourist website. It's one of this island's few attractions. Those things can't have been chucking every country walker into the sea."

"No, only those with magical ability approaching the mage's house with ill intent," Cassandra said.

Sebastian cocked his head. "Ill intent?"

"We do intend to break in, don't we?" Cassandra asked.

"Yes, I suppose that's on the agenda," Sebastian said with a sigh. "But it's not as if some spirit could detect that."

Della had to smile. Her poor ex had no idea what he had gotten into.

They carried on. The house stood over the next rise.

At first sight, it looked unremarkable, a low stone structure with a slate roof. It did look older than most of the houses they had seen on the islands, probably an early crofter's cottage. It had a single story and an attic under the gable roof. Perhaps a cellar, although Della certainly wasn't going to volunteer to explore that. It was only on a second look that some unusual elements became noticeable.

Firstly, there was no road to it, only a rutted muddy track. The only visible road cut across the next valley, nearly a kilometer away. No vehicle was parked outside. The windows were boarded up. There was no garden, no ornamentation, nothing. Della got the impression of an abandoned movie set.

"MacHugh wasn't much on home decoration," Della said.

"He was a true recluse, from what I've heard," Richard said. "I never met the man. In fact, I've never met anyone who met him. Montague only took his postal orders. The chap didn't even have internet."

"So how do we do this?" Della asked, looking around. The terrain was open grassland or farmer's fields, utterly treeless. While there were only a few houses, and none nearby, they were completely visible to anyone who bothered to look.

Lucas was studying his map again. "According to this, the trail continues past his house on the seaward side, sticking close to the cliff." He was interrupted by a groan from Sebastian. "We can continue to pretend we're country walkers and go along the path. It will get us close to his house, and we can see what to do from there."

"Country walkers out in the rain in Orkney in winter?" Cassandra asked.

Lucas shrugged. Cassandra didn't suggest any better ideas. Della couldn't think of any either.

As the map promised, the path kept them within a few meters of the cliff. Della watched the house as they approached. All the ground floor windows were boarded up. Only a little attic window under the gable still had its glass uncovered. The front door had a chain and padlock on it, and someone had stuck a red-and-white No Trespassing notice on it.

"So, do you think MacHugh put those trolls on the bridge?" she asked.

Immediately after the words came out of her mouth, she cringed and glanced at Sebastian. She still wasn't used to saying seemingly ridiculous statements like that.

Sebastian, though, only trudged along, looking at the ground and lost in his thoughts.

"I don't think so," Richard said. "Any wards he placed would have been on the house. It would have taken quite a lot of power to put such spirits on the bridge and all other approaches. As you can see, people can come at this house from any direction. We just chose the most dangerous. No, there's something else going on."

"Something to do with that taint in the ley lines?"

"Perhaps, although there are none through this island. I find that curious."

"Curious as in you can't explain it?"

"Curious as in there are so many possible explanations, both the ones I know and the ones I don't, that there's no point trying to theorize at the moment."

Della glanced at Cassandra, who gave a resigned nod. As much as Della disliked the rich girl, she did know as much about these things as Richard, and far more than anyone else in the group.

Della allowed herself an ironic smile. So the occultists were using a bit of the scientific method, waiting until they had more evidence before trying to come up with a conclusion. When she had first been introduced to this strange world, she had not expected that sort of logical thinking about illogical things.

Keeping to the path, they got as close as they could to the house. With the house now between them and much of the surrounding countryside, they felt confident moving to the near side of the house without too much chance of someone spotting them. Della kept glancing up at that little window beneath the eaves, half expecting to see an ugly face wearing a red cap leering down on them.

This side had one ground floor window, boarded up like the rest. Della wondered if this was where the last burglars had tried to get in.

Those two locals had been spotted, and now here they were, a whole group of strangers in broad daylight trying to do the same thing.

"Maybe this isn't such a good idea," Della said.

Sebastian put a hand on her shoulder and quietly said, "You're right. Let them go in if they want to. Stay out here with me."

She looked around again. The rain had eased, and the clear spot out to sea had grown closer, increasing visibility. She didn't see anyone watching them, but that didn't mean there wasn't.

Richard and Lucas didn't seem worried. They moved to the boards, and Lucas pulled a claw hammer out of his pocket.

"Do you always go on trips with a hammer?" Sebastian asked.

"Not until recently."

It only took a few seconds to pry the board off its wooden frame.

"This is illegal," Sebastian whispered to Della.

"There are larger issues at stake."

Lucas tried the window, found it locked, and pulled out a slim piece of metal. With it, he was able to flip the catch and open the window. He then pushed it up. Richard made a step out of his hands and helped Lucas climb through. Lucas immediately reappeared and grabbed Richard's arm, pulling him up.

Sebastian looked appalled. "Do these two make a regular habit of this sort of thing?"

"Sadly, yes," Richard said over his shoulder as he wormed through the window. "Lucas is quite the handyman."

Lucas reappeared again, holding his hand out to Della. Over Sebastian's objections, she crawled through the window.

None of them expected what they found in there.

18

LUCAS REALLY, really wished Sebastian would stop talking. He did not find him amusing, or witty, and now that he had been awakened to the reality of the hidden world, he wouldn't stop yammering on about how dangerous this all was. As if he was the only one running a risk here.

Granted, the chap had just gone through a major change in his worldview, but he didn't have to be such a moaner about it.

A curious moaner, though. Lucas had to grant him that. After it became apparent that not even Cassandra had a problem crawling through a window into someone else's house, he followed. Sebastian didn't want to be the odd man out.

It would have been better for the poor bastard if he had.

Because as soon as they got inside, they could feel it.

There was a coldness to the place, a subtle menace that they couldn't ignore.

Not anything physical, at least not yet.

Visually, everything looked normal, even mundane. They had crawled through the window and over a sink into the kitchen. It was a simple place with an old flagstone floor, a throw rug to keep it from being too cold, and old-fashioned wallpaper. An old iron stove stood to one side along with several cupboards. It looked like MacHugh hadn't redecorated in fifty years.

Everyone turned on the flashlights on their phones. Their surroundings, now brightly lit, still felt grim and foreboding.

The kitchen door was closed. Lucas really, really did not want to explore the rest of the house, but he knew they must.

Squaring his shoulders, he opened the door. It led to a hall, as dank and quiet as the kitchen. Doors led off it to either side and in front. All were closed. Somehow the idea of all the doors being closed in an abandoned house disturbed him.

They chose the right-hand one and found it led to a large living room and library, or what had once been such. The floor-to-ceiling shelves were all bare, and the furniture lay shrouded in white cloth, looking like squat ghosts in the light of their mobile phones. He noticed several spots where furniture clearly had been removed by the scuffs they had left on the wooden floor after years of use. He pulled up a cloth on one of the remaining pieces and saw it was modern. Probably the missing ones had been older, like the house, and had been sold off. The modern pieces had little resale value.

"I wonder what hung on the walls," Della said. Even though she whispered, her voice sounded loud in the silent room and made Lucas cringe.

Relax, he told himself. *There's no one here to hear.*

At least no one corporeal.

There were several lighter spots on the old wall-paper where pictures had once hung. Nothing was on the wall now.

"There's nothing in here either," Cassandra said. She had crossed the hallway to check out the left-hand room.

Lucas followed her and found a modest bedroom. If the bed hadn't still been there, Lucas would not have been able to tell the room's function. Everything else had been removed. The bed had a special, expensive osteopathic mattress. So the great occultist Frederick MacHugh had suffered from a bad back. Lucas smiled. That made him more human somehow.

When Lucas and Cassandra emerged from the bedroom, having first checked under the bed and finding only dust, Richard was already opening the third door. It led to another short hallway and the front door. Off to the side was a small sitting room and a steep set of wooden stairs leading to a hatch in the ceiling.

Lucas stopped and looked at it, letting out a sigh.

Richard nudged him and grinned. "You first."

"Why?"

"Because in monster movies the black guy always gets killed first. It's time for a change."

"Very funny."

"Climb those stairs and show Della what a dashingly brave man you are."

Lucas glanced at Della, who shrugged.

"I can go if you want."

"No." Lucas sighed again. "I'll do it."

He climbed the steep, narrow steps. They were of old wood and probably original to the house, which Lucas judged to be seventeenth or eighteenth century. Taking a deep breath, he pressed his hand against the wooden hatch and pushed it open.

The sense of foul magic was stronger up here. Shining the light from his phone ahead of him, he poked his head up to look inside the attic.

Unlike the rest of the house, this part had not been cleared at all. Inside was a jumble of things like one usually found in an attic—some old toys, including a rocking horse that seem to glare at him in the light of his phone, several cardboard boxes, and an old lamp and birdcage.

But what struck him most was the line of shoes hanging by their laces from the rafters.

They ran the length of the attic, from one end of the house to the other.

The magic was coming from them. He could sense it.

Lucas eased back down the stairs, his heart racing.

"MacHugh did some apotropaic magic up there," he said once he got back down to his friends. Having them crowd around him made him feel a bit safer. Not much, but it helped.

"What's that?" Sebastian asked.

"Magic to stop harmful influences, like evil spells

or witches. There's a bunch of old shoes up there hanging from the rafter. And before you say anything, yes, old shoes can trap spirits and witches. It's not the shoes themselves but the spell associated with them."

Sebastian hung his head and didn't reply. After the fight on the natural bridge, Lucas didn't think he'd be getting many more arguments out of him.

Cassandra climbed the narrow steps, took one look, and quickly came back down.

"Whatever he was trying to stop coming into this house, it looks like he caught it."

"Maybe the same group that sent a spirit after those books tried to get them while they were still here, after MacHugh died and before they got sold to Montague," Della said.

The others nodded, except for Sebastian, who looked lost.

"We shouldn't disturb the upstairs," Lucas said.

"But what if there's something up there we need to see? Maybe some clue?" Della asked.

"We don't want to risk disturbing what's up there," Lucas said, his voice firmer this time. He looked to Richard and Cassandra, and to his profound relief, he saw no disagreement.

A crash in the kitchen made them spin around.

Richard moved to the door.

"I'll handle this," he said, pulling out the brass amulet he carried. Lucas had learned it was two hundred years old, was inscribed with a complex pattern of sigils, and could be used as a focal point for many spells. Lucas got behind him, ready to back his friend up but preferring to have that amulet between him and whatever was in the kitchen.

His faith in an old disk of brass plummeted when the door banged open and they were confronted by a scowling man in a yellow raincoat pointing a shotgun at them.

Richard raised his hands. "Please don't be an American!"

The man glanced at the disk in Richard's hand then studied him and Lucas for a second. His gaze flicked beyond them, noticing the others in the room, then he demanded in a local accent, "Who are you? What are you doing here?"

Nobody answered. Lucas tried to come up with a plausible excuse for their presence and drew a blank. Staring down the barrel of a shotgun did not help his creativity.

The man gestured with the gun. "Talk. You're practitioners, from the look of that amulet in your hand."

Lucas relaxed slightly. This man was not the police or some gun-crazy local ready to blast their heads off at a moment's notice. Now that he could focus more, Lucas detected some Talent on him.

That meant they could talk frankly.

But that might be a really bad idea.

Before Lucas could come up with something, Richard decided honesty was the best policy.

"There's something wrong with the ley lines. I'm thinking you're not responsible for that, seeing as you haven't pulled the trigger."

The man's eyes narrowed. "Go on."

"We are all practitioners with the Talent, as I'm sure you've sensed. We came here to find out why the lye lines are disturbed," Richard said.

"Which one of you is that bookseller? I can hear you have a London accent."

"Good ear, darling."

Lucas gritted his teeth. *Don't call a man darling when he has a gun trained on you.*

"You the bookseller?" the man repeated. That gun hadn't budged.

"He's not with us."

"Why not?"

Lucas wondered how much this man really knew. While Montague's name had been kept out of the papers, news of his death had spread quickly through London's occult community. He had assumed it had spread farther.

"He's dead, and I've been made trustee of his estate. Mind lowering that gun so we can chat more amicably?"

"There's nothing here for you. MacHugh's kinfolk took everything."

"Then why did someone try breaking in here a month ago?" Lucas asked.

The man looked confused. "No one's been doing that."

Lucas cocked his head. "You sure?"

The gun swiveled in his direction. "Sure I'm sure. I live just down the hill. I've been keeping an eye on the place."

"But we read a report of a break-in," Lucas said, trying to keep his voice calm while staring at the baleful black eye of the shotgun's barrel. "Two people were arrested."

The man shook his head. "You got it wrong. I'd know."

"Did we trip a ward?" Lucas asked.

The man smiled. "You sure did. The English don't know all the tricks."

"I'm British, darling," Richard said.

Stop calling him darling!

"Whatever you are, I want more of an explanation than you've given."

Lucas glanced up at the attic. "Can we speak somewhere safer? There are several spirits or curses trapped in shoes in the attic."

The man took in this information in the same way he might have if Lucas had said there was a leak in the roof.

"All right. We can go back to my house. It's close."

If you're inviting us to your house, does that mean you're going to stop pointing a gun at us?

It didn't, at least not at first. He stood to one side of the kitchen as they climbed through the window one by one. He warned them not to run off, saying they were trapped on the island until the evening ferry and he knew every corner of the place. Lucas believed him. And as intimidating as this man was, Lucas did not think they were in any danger as long as they behaved. At this point, he looked more curious than threatening.

Once they were all out, he asked how they had pried open the window. Lucas produced the hammer, and the man ordered him to nail the board back on the frame. Lucas didn't like making so much noise, but he didn't see anyone else around and the wind and rain had picked up, muffling the sound.

"My house is just down in the glen there."

They started to walk. The man walked a few paces behind them. At least he had slung his shotgun.

Della moved close beside Lucas. "I thought you weren't allowed to own guns in the UK," she whispered.

"People in rural areas can. Unfortunately."

Lucas got the impression that the local was waiting for them to talk, so he talked.

"Our friend the bookseller, Montague Summers, was killed by a spirit summoning down in London. My friend here is selling the books now, as he mentioned, but someone summoned a fire spirit from Maeshowe to try and steal them. That's why we're up here."

The man cursed under his breath.

"Do you know who might have done that?" Lucas asked.

"I suspect I do," the man said grimly.

He did not elaborate for the rest of the long walk to his house.

It was a little cottage next to a field where a flock of sheep clustered together against the elements. A vegetable garden stood to one side. The man let them in, and they sat in a small living room. It was crowded with all of them in there, but at least it was warm and dry.

A two-way radio on a small desk in one corner crackled.

"Wind force six from north-northwest. Holding steady," a voice said.

"What's that?" Lucas asked.

"Marine radio," the man said. "I'm a fisherman."

He stood in the entrance hall with his arms crossed. Although he had put his gun against the wall, his heavy frame blocked the exit.

He did not look like he was going to offer up any more information, so Lucas struggled to figure out how much to reveal.

Once again, Sebastian made the decision for him.

"We were attacked on the natural bridge. I nearly got shoved off it."

"What did they look like?" the fisherman asked.

Sebastian shuddered and looked at the floor.

They, Lucas thought. *He said they. He knows it was trolls.*

"The *genius loci* of these islands, taking on the semblance of trolls," Lucas said. "We got attacked in

Maeshowe by them, too, and nearly attacked in our Airbnb."

The fisherman let out a low, slow breath through clenched teeth.

"They've done it. The bastards have done it. I tried to stop them, tried to warn them, and now this."

"You could tell us what you know?" Della pleaded. "Perhaps we could be of help."

He studied her. Then his cold blue eyes studied each person in the room.

"You first," he said at last. "Tell me everything."

And so they did. Sebastian paled at some of the accounts but contributed his share of observations. When they finally finished, the fisherman nodded and started to speak.

"My name is James Firth. I've lived in this house all my life. As MacHugh's closest neighbor, and the only one with the Talent, I got to know him better than anyone, although I can't say I knew him well. When he died, I took it upon myself to watch over the house. I knew people would come up to cause trouble."

"Did they?" Lucas asked.

"Not at all. I don't know where you heard that."

"On a chat forum." Lucas pulled out his phone. "I'm not getting a signal. Do you have Wi-Fi?"

James smiled and shook his head. "There's no need for that here. Whatever you read on the internet is a lie. You shouldn't be surprised by that."

"Why would someone lie about two people being arrested for trying to break into MacHugh's house?"

Lucas glanced at Sebastian, who stared fixedly at the fisherman and did not acknowledge him.

James shrugged. "Who knows? The internet is full of nonsense, especially in those pages where they claim to talk about the Craft. You should know that by now. But as I was saying, the next of kin came up quickly enough and cleared everything out. They may not have known MacHugh very well, but they knew his library was worth a fortune. Swept in like seagulls around a fresh catch. It was only afterward that the trouble started."

"Trouble?" Richard asked.

"It started shortly after MacHugh's death. I felt strange fluctuations in the ley lines anytime I went to Mainland or any of the larger islands. And a growing taint. I'm sure you've felt it. I had heard rumors that MacHugh had been working on a ritual to summon up the *genius loci* in certain sacred sites around the islands. He was a traditionalist, set in the old ways."

Lucas glanced around the room, which, except

for the light bulb and the marine radio, didn't look much different than it must have looked a hundred years before, and realized that if James called someone a traditionalist, they most certainly were.

James Firth went on.

"He wanted to revive the beliefs here in the islands, get people back to the way things used to be. We have a lot of incomers, you see. Decent enough folk, the bulk of them, but they're not from here and don't know the islands the way an islander does. MacHugh wanted to change that. He wanted to *show* them."

"Show them what?" Lucas asked.

The fisherman's eyes lit up. "The spirits that make these islands their home. The trolls and the selkie, the ghosts and the cunning women. All the lost legacy of magic that's fading in the modern world with your bloody phones and your bloody electronic music. The world is dying. You don't have to stare at the internet all day to know that. Trees being cut and animals disappearing and poison put into our air and water like there's no tomorrow. No one is connected to the land or the sea anymore, so we wreck them. He wanted to show people the world as it really is, get them to appreciate it more, respect it."

Lucas studied him for a moment. James looked ecstatic. "And so he did what, exactly?"

"A powerful ritual, and a very old one. It's meant to activate the ley lines so much that the spirits manifest in this world like they never can normally. That's why you've been seeing so many trolls. Out on the sea, I've seen selkies. At night, I've seen ghosts passing along the old paths. And it's getting stronger."

"Too strong," Richard said. "I don't like ugly little creatures trying to push my friends off cliffs. And what's that taint we're sensing in the ley lines?"

James grimaced. "Too much of a good thing. MacHugh used ritual magic to stimulate the ley lines. The idea was to put power into the system to make more of the hidden world manifest. He wanted people to spot the spirits of the land and feel some of the area's magic for themselves. We've lost touch all over the world. Here's one of the places where we're still a bit closer to the real magic of the earth. He wanted people to reconnect with that. The problem is, he died shortly thereafter, and it's an ongoing spell. Once set, it continues. It's like when you go to the doctor and they use that little hammer to test your reflexes. No harm in that. Gets a reaction. But that hammer has been banging away on the knee for weeks now. The knee isn't just reacting now, it's thrashing in pain. Sooner or later, it's going to break."

"Well, stop it!" Sebastian said.

James shook his head. "This spell isn't like a computer, boy. You can't just switch it off. I wanted to do a ritual on MacHugh's body to get his aid from the other side to stop the spell, but I nearly got caught breaking into the morgue. The police kept a watch on the place until he was cremated, and I didn't get another chance. By then the damage had been done. MacHugh set a spell in motion that no practitioner on the islands is strong enough to stop."

"Aren't they even trying?" Lucas asked.

"No, many aren't. They're looking after their own skins. Or they don't know enough to see the danger we're all in. Or they're trying but too weak."

"One group sent a fire demon after us to get some of MacHugh's books to protect themselves from this," Richard said.

James made a face. "That would be the Stromness group, down on Mainland. Looking after themselves and no one else. They've always been that way. We'll get no help from them."

"Do you think they might have murdered MacHugh?"

"No. They don't have the strength or the daring.

No reason to do so, either. While they're acting selfishly now, they don't want to be in this mess any more than we do. They won't help, though. They're like the man on a sinking ship who grabs all the life preservers for himself."

"This is my dream," Della whispered.

James turned to her.

"I dreamt my dead bookseller friend was pouring beer into the top of a burial mound. He turned to me and said that I have to feed them but to be careful not to feed them too much."

James nodded. "Your friend was trying to teach you an important lesson from the Beyond. He must have known what MacHugh was planning. Maybe he figured it out from some books MacHugh bought from him."

"What can we do?" Della asked.

James shook his head slowly. "I'm not sure we can do anything. We can try to lay the spell to rest, but that means a ritual in Maeshowe."

"We almost didn't survive our last visit there," Lucas said.

Della, sitting next to him, shuddered.

James looked at each of them in turn. "There's something else we need. It was an Orcadian spell that MacHugh set up to do this, and we need an

Orcadian spell to lay it to rest. The problem is, we need two people initiated into the Orcadian Rite in order to perform it. I know some initiates who can help, but none are powerful enough."

"I'd be honored to be initiated," Richard said. "I specialize in fusing different spiritual paths together and have been initiated into several traditions."

James shook his head. "I appreciate the offer, but we need to initiate the strongest among you."

Richard cocked an eyebrow. "And who might that be?"

The fisherman pointed at Della. "Her."

Della's jaw dropped. She looked for a moment at Lucas, then back at James. "I'll do whatever I can to help," she said.

"We all will," Lucas said.

James studied him for a moment. "You're powerful. I can feel that clearly enough. That Yank's got the most potential, and the fancy man and the toff look like they know what they're doing. This other fellow's got an odd power to him. Not quite sure about him. You're a strange crew, though, all mixed up. Surprised you are bunched together the way you are. Think you can do what's required?"

"It depends on what's required," Lucas said.

James snorted. "Oh, it won't be pretty."

The radio crackled again. "Northlink ferry to Whitehall port. Docking in five minutes. Please send a security officer to the docks and do not allow anyone to board. Repeat, do not allow anyone to board. Two officers from Kirkwall are on board coming to arrest several suspects. Be on the lookout for two Anglo males in their late twenties, two Anglo females in their early twenties, and one Afro-Caribbean male in his late forties. They are suspected of breaking into a private residence in Stronsay."

Lucas stared at the radio and then at James Firth.

The fisherman looked equally surprised. "I didn't call them. And I doubt anyone else saw you. Wait a minute, you only broke in an hour ago. They couldn't have gotten here in that time."

Lucas blinked. Then how could they have known?

He turned to Sebastian.

The only people who knew their intentions were sitting in this room, and the only person he didn't know well was Sebastian.

But would he inform the police that he planned to commit a crime? It didn't make any sense.

Lucas couldn't figure it out.

He would, though. Oh yes, he would.

19

HOW COULD the police have known about them?

The question ran around and around in Della's mind as they sat cramped on the deck of James's fishing boat. There wasn't room in the cabin for all of them. James stood inside at the wheel, and Cassandra had gone in there with him. There was no more room for anyone else.

So the rest of them sat uncomfortably on coils of rope and bunches of netting as the rain and the waves sprayed in their faces. The sea was rough but not dangerously so. It was the least of Della's worries.

She couldn't understand how the police could have known their intentions, unless some mage had divined it and tipped them off to stop them from getting rid of the spell.

Could it have been that circle in Stromness James had mentioned? They didn't seem to care what happened to anyone else. But why would they actively try to stop them? That made no sense.

The question remained unanswerable. The main problem was stopping the spell, and that would require being initiated.

Her dream was coming true. In her sleep, Della had seen a woman getting initiated in the Orcadian Rite. She had never suspected that it had been a projection of herself.

Della trembled. For the past few months, this new reality had slowly been soaking into her consciousness. The violent episodes in Oxford and London had terrified her and forced her to rethink everything she thought she knew about the world. But it had been the quieter times, the times she had cloistered herself in her apartment, that had really allowed her to accept this new reality. Aunt Mary had patiently been lending her a series of books to read. At first, Della had read them with scoffing amusement. That had been a façade, though, a defense mechanism. A last-ditch effort of her consciousness to reject having to completely change its worldview. As she read more and more that made sense of her terrifying and undeniable experiences, however, she began to accept what she read with a fearful resignation.

And then something strange happened. Something that she should have recognized as an old habit in a new situation.

She began to study occultism like any other subject. For hours she'd read through increasingly complex texts, weighing the strength of various theories of magic, tracing the lineages of certain rites, and prying out the details of ancient practices from vague and often contradictory sources. Della even toyed with the idea of writing an academic article about the contribution of ancient beliefs to modern occult practices. Leaving out the fact that it was all true, of course.

Della had turned it into a course of study. Like archaeology or laboratory techniques or Old English.

But it wasn't a course of study. It was a bunch of survival techniques. It was manipulating power to get what you wanted or save your own life.

Or everybody's lives.

Now she saw why she had so readily let Aunt Mary ply her with books. Books were familiar. Safe. Even when they were about real things, they had a comfortable detachment from reality.

Like her life, most of the time.

But she couldn't enjoy a state of intellectual detachment from her new reality. Not anymore.

She had read enough to know what initiation into any rite involved. It meant presenting yourself to the spirit world and vowing to have a deep connection with it. It meant giving up pretending this was a mental game and getting into it for real.

It meant taking a final step she had never thought would be asked of her.

She needed to talk with James.

Della stood, taking the wide-legged stance she had seen the stewardess take on their stormy flight, and waddled to the cabin.

Cassandra was at the wheel. James was standing close behind her—way too close, with his arms around her and guiding her hands.

"I tell you, girlie, you're a natural! Water magic is your Talent, sure as sunrise."

Della couldn't help but smile. Cassandra had finally found a man who would pay attention to her. Of course it was a man in his forties who, a couple of hours ago, had been pointing a shotgun at them, but obviously Cassandra was too eager for attention to care.

"Excuse me," Della said, blushing. Interrupting them felt pretty awkward.

James and Cassandra looked over their shoulders.

"Oh hey, you want a turn at the wheel?" James asked.

Cassandra elbowed him. "She'll drown us all, you silly man."

"I need to talk with you about the initiation," Della said, feeling her face go scarlet.

"Bah!" Cassandra untangled herself from the fisherman, who quickly took hold of the wheel. "All work and no play."

She left the cabin so Della would have room to enter.

"Why did you pick me?" Della asked.

"You're the most powerful, like I said," James said, not taking his eyes off the rough sea.

"I had a dream about this. I dreamt of a woman lying on a beach at night, weighed down by seven stones. She cried out, 'To thee! To thee! In your domain between the land and the sea!'"

James nodded. "That's the ritual. You're fated to do it."

"What does it mean? Who was the woman speaking to?"

"The spirits. There are spirits of the land and of the sea. Proclaiming yourself connected to them in a spot that's both land and sea makes you aligned with both."

Della felt a chill. "And then what?"

James looked her over for a moment before going back to steering the ship.

"Then you become a practitioner for real. You're new, aren't you?"

Della nodded. "Very new. I didn't even know about this stuff six months ago. A lot has happened since then."

James nodded. "Yes, I can see that. I can see that as plain as day. It's a pity. We need you because you're the most powerful, but I won't lie to you. It's dangerous to do what you need to do without any real knowledge."

"There was a third part of my dream. One I haven't mentioned."

"Tell me."

"It was a playground with a bunch of children. They were all laughing at a girl with a crow's head. The girl looked upset and clutched her head and let out a cry. Then a woman came through the crowd and shouted at her for not remembering something she had been taught. She slapped the girl, and her head turned back to normal."

The fisherman let out a long, low whistle. "You

really do have the Sight, don't you? That's an old Orkney folktale."

"Tell me about it."

"Well, it's pretty much as you told it. A witch woman is teaching her little girl the Craft, and the girl gets to boasting to her little friends that she can do all sorts of magic. They don't believe her, and to show off, she turns herself into a crow. Except she didn't remember the whole spell for getting back into human form."

Della nodded, her heart going cold. "It's a warning. A warning not to overextend your magical knowledge."

"That's right."

"And now I have to get initiated and help stop a spell started by someone who had way more power and knowledge than I do."

"Don't worry. I'll be with you every step of the way."

Something in the water to her left caught her eye. The gray hump of a seal undulated through the waves. Della studied it. She was no expert, but it looked a bit strange for a seal, long and too thin. It kept moving, and its movements looked odd, more like a person swimming than an animal.

The creature poked its head above the water and

looked directly at the boat. Della's breath caught. It had the face of a man!

A moment later it was gone. She blinked. Had she truly seen it?

The radio in the boat crackled. Someone said something in a foreign language. James picked up the microphone and replied in the same language. Della didn't even look at him. She was still scanning the waves, hoping for another glimpse of the thing.

A distant horn sounded off to their left. Della spotted another fishing boat close to the horizon. James laughed, sounded his own horn, and said something over the radio.

The language sounded familiar. Scandinavian, but with a different, harsher tone to it.

"Is that... Old Norse?"

"That's right," James said, giving her an admiring look. "Cassandra mentioned you're a student of history. Some of us have kept the old ways here."

"What does the harbormaster think when he hears Old Norse over the radio?"

The fisherman chuckled. "He thinks we're part of a folklore group. We put on shows and museum exhibits for the tourists. Not many know what we really do."

"Who's that in the other boat?"

"Reinforcements. More are coming. Don't worry, you won't be on your own."

"Glad to hear it."

James's face went grim. "You should be. If you had to do this on your own, I doubt you'd survive. And if you did, you probably wouldn't want to."

Della went cold. She looked out at the rough sea, where in the distance she could see the low hills of Mainland. They'd be there soon. The light was already fading. Soon it would be time for her initiation. And then…

She shuddered, leaving the cabin to take refuge with her friends in the rain.

"Send Cassandra back," James called over his shoulder. "If we're all going to die, I'd like to get my fun while I can."

Della relayed everything she had heard. Everyone listened in grim silence, even Cassandra. When she finished, Della asked, "Do you think it's all true? Can we trust him?"

Lucas nodded. "Yes, it all makes sense. If he was one of those who sent the fire demon at us, he could have shot us back in the house or called the police. I think we have to do it his way."

"Local magic caused this thing," Cassandra said, "and it will take local magic to put it down."

Della felt a tug of despair. So she'd have to go through with it. She'd have to be initiated. She'd finally have to face the fact that she was fully part of this secret world.

She had been able to ignore it for much of this trip. There had always been something to distract her—Cassandra flirting with Lucas, Sebastian being weird, meeting Bjorn, seeing some amazing ancient sights, even the terrible weather.

All of those things had been petty, though. Minor incidents of a mundane life. It had given her mind something to fix on instead of the vast danger that faced them all and the central role she had to take in order to fix it.

Richard and Cassandra began to plan strategy, speaking in esoteric terms that went right over Della's head. Lucas didn't look like he understood either. Sebastian sat there huddled in his raincoat looking as miserable as Della felt.

By the time they docked, three other fishing boats were visible behind them. One was the boat that had blown its horn at them. The other two had appeared within half an hour. Everyone docked, and James showed Lucas on his map where they needed to meet.

A spot on the beach a few miles away, far from any settlement.

Della knew what would come next.

James did not come with them, nor any of the other fishermen who were docking and pretending like their simultaneous arrival had just been coincidence. Della and her companions climbed into the rental car and drove slowly away.

Sebastian sat next to her in the back.

"I'm sorry," he said.

"For what?"

"For getting you into this. If I hadn't suggested going to MacHugh's house, none of this would have ever happened."

Della looked at him with surprise. It was a ridiculous statement. "But things are turning out for the best. We met who we needed to meet."

Sebastian shook his head. "I don't think so."

"It's a synchronicity, darling," Richard said. "You need to appreciate those."

"Are all synchronicities good?" Sebastian asked, hanging his head and still looking guilty.

Lucas glanced at him through the rearview mirror.

Richard didn't have an answer to that.

The quick northern dusk was well finished by

the time they made it to the spot James had indicated, and Lucas pulled the car off a quiet road and into a field by the shine of his headlights. When he switched those off, they were in darkness.

They got out of the car into a grassy field. A cold drizzle stung their faces with icy droplets. Della could hear the distant sound of surf and smell the sea.

The others did not take long. Two cars and a pickup truck came in file, as if in military formation, and parked behind them. Men and women in rain gear piled out, not speaking. James strode up to them. As he did so, the last person from the last car closed his door, cutting off the last of the light. James remained visible as only a darker shadow against the prevailing gloom.

"Are you ready?" James asked her.

"No."

"Do you know what you're getting into?"

"No."

"Will you trust yourself to fate and your own abilities?"

Della paused and then, against her better judgment, said, "Yes."

She thought she saw him nod but wasn't sure. "Those are the correct answers. Let's go."

Without another word, he moved off across the field, his fellow Orcadians falling in with him. Della stood by the road for a moment, unsure of herself, then hurried to catch up. Her friends did as well.

Everyone kept silent as they drew closer to the sea. Della wanted to ask James a thousand questions but felt too afraid to speak. She knew she wouldn't have liked the answers.

The field sloped down to a narrow beach. The wind was colder here, sending the rain into her face like icy needles.

As they passed through the tall grass that clung to the boundary between the field and beach, Della's eyes widened. The beach was softly glowing as if under moonlight, and yet the sky was overcast. The sea, too, had a pale, bone-white glow. Her skin prickled as she felt magic flow through her.

"Are we on a ley line?" she whispered. She didn't dare speak in a normal voice. It would have been like shouting in a cathedral.

"No," James said.

"I didn't think so. It feels... different."

"The way old MacHugh's spell has been going, we don't need to be on a ley line anymore. But we don't have much time. If the lines get much stronger, they'll right themselves, and God help us all."

"When will that happen?"

"Nobody knows. Soon, at any rate."

"Tomorrow? Next week?"

"Next week is too far out. Perhaps tomorrow. Perhaps tonight. I noticed you staring at that selkie."

Della didn't reply. She couldn't deny what she saw, and yet knew she'd feel like a fool saying she had seen the northern equivalent of a mermaid.

They walked onto the beach, their footsteps leaving eerie dark footprints in the shining sand. James's companions spread out, some moving off to either side to act as lookouts. Della thought she spotted a few carrying guns. James, her companions, and some others walked to the edge of the surf, where the sand shone a bit brighter and was packed hard and damp. Without a word, they formed a silent circle around her.

Della moved into the center, heart beating fast. She looked around at those facing inward toward her. To her relief, she spotted Lucas and Richard and Cassandra. After a moment's hesitation, Sebastian joined the circle.

Taking a deep breath, she lay down on the sand. Some of the Orcadians moved into the center of the circle, carrying stones that they set on her arms and legs and chest.

Panic rose up in her as they moved back. She stared up at the black sky, feeling the crackling power of magic flowing through her. If she did this, she would never be able to go back.

If she didn't do it, she and all those she held dear might not live to see the end of the week.

"Are you willing?" James called out.

Della licked her lips and tried to reply. Her throat was so dry her voice came out as a harsh croak. For a moment it sounded like a crow squawking. She cleared her throat and spoke in as strong of a voice as she could muster.

"Yes."

The Orcadians in the circle began to chant in Old Norse, and Della entered a new phase of her life, one from which she could never return.

20

LUCAS DIDN'T KNOW how an Orcadian initiation rite was supposed to go, but he was pretty sure it wasn't supposed to have seal men wading out of the sea.

As Lucas tried to focus his will to help with a ritual he did not know, he was torn between worry for Della and a lingering mistrust of these Orcadians. While he did not think this was a trap, it was this sort of ritual magic that had led to the problem in the first place. It was a bit like letting an alcoholic manage your pub.

Whatever he might have thought of the ritual, there was no denying its power. How could it not be powerful with this crackling of magical energy all around them? He could feel the circle draw in that ambient energy and focus it in on Della, who lay in the sand, eyes bugging, staring at the sky.

Lucas happened to be facing the sea, and so he was one of the first to see the dozen or so dark forms emerge from the phosphorescent water and move toward the shore.

Others had been keeping watch too. Several of the Orcadian practitioners quickly moved to form a line between the circle and the sea. They raised their arms in unison and began to chant.

The forms hesitated as if unsure of themselves. Silhouetted as the intruders were against the softly glowing water, he could see they had the shapes of men, with overly long arms and webbed hands. Lucas had to struggle to maintain his focus on the ritual.

Selkie, he thought. *The* genius loci *are taking the shape of selkie, just like they've taken the shape of trolls. This is part of the ley system trying to protect itself.*

And it will only get worse.

The dark forms advanced to the shallows. The protective line of humans between them and the circle rose their voices. Lucas could feel the force of magic rippling off them as if it were forming a wall.

At the same time, he felt the strength of the circle weaken.

His fault, and perhaps the fault of others who got distracted by the spiritual battle happening not five paces away.

To practice magic, one must learn to focus, Aunt Mary always used to say. *No matter what happens around you, no matter what you see or hear or feel, the safest thing you can do is focus on the task before you.*

She had said that many times as he was growing up, and as with everything else she'd said about magic, he had listened with only half an ear, like when she had told him that he was inheriting her magical strength.

Aunt Mary had repeated these things because they had been important.

I've never accepted my power because of Mum and Dad, he realized. *Now I need to, or I'll end up like them.*

We'll all end up like them.

Closing his eyes to shut out the battle in the shallows, from which came the sound of screaming and thrashing, he focused his willpower on the band of magical energy flowing inward to Della. Distantly he heard her cry out the words of power that would initiate her into a rite she had never heard of before today and would result in her becoming one of a group of practitioners of an art she barely understood and could not control.

And yet it was necessary.

It would be for him, too, but not tonight.

There was too much else to do.

A pulse of energy made him jerk. The ritual had reached a tipping point. It was as if an entire bathtub of liquid energy had poured down the drain all at once.

Right into Della.

Lucas heard Della cry out. His eyes snapped open just in time to see her leap to her feet, the stones holding her down thumping to the sand. James shouted something in Old Norse that sounded like a triumphant battle cry.

Della whirled around and faced the selkie, which dove back into the water and disappeared in a heartbeat.

But not soon enough to save everyone in that thin line protecting the ritual circle. Several of the Orcadians lay unmoving in the surf, unconscious or dead.

Lucas staggered, stunned by the power of the force that had just rushed through him. How Della could be on her feet baffled him. He could feel the power sparking off her.

She turned to him. Through a strange trick of the phosphorescence, he could see her face clearly.

She looked equal parts ecstatic and terrified.

"We need to get to Maeshowe right now," she said. "The ley lines felt this ritual and are reacting to it like a threat. They're going to scale up more quickly."

Lucas didn't feel anything different, but he sure wasn't going to argue with someone who had more power emanating off of them than anyone he had ever met.

James didn't argue either. With a few curt words, he ordered some of the group to stay and see if they could help the injured, while the rest hurried back to the cars.

Lucas and Richard fell in beside James. Della ran a bit apart. Lucas sensed she wanted to be alone. Her mind must be a whirl of new sensations and insights. Lucas sure felt that way himself.

"So how do we handle this?" Richard asked James. "I presume you have a bolt cutter or something to get us through that metal door?"

"We do," the fisherman replied. "But it's not that simple. One of my friends drinks with an officer at Kirkwall, and he was saying they think the fire at Maeshowe was arson."

"It wasn't. It was the spirits coming after us," Lucas said.

"You know that. I know that. The police are looking for some mundane solution. We can't rely on them for help. From what I heard, they're going to start patrolling the area tonight. We'll have to take care."

"If I remember correctly, there's only one road there. They can watch it easily."

"We'll stop at a place I know and cut across the fields."

"What about the ley lines?" Richard asked. "We're going to have to step on one when we go to the burial mound."

"I know," James whispered.

"And what will happen when we do?" Richard asked.

That question made his heart clench. He had never known Richard to not know the answer to a question on occultism.

"I have no idea," James said, his voice wavering a little.

To hear such a solid man sound frightened made Lucas feel even worse.

Lucas made sure to sit by Della on the drive over. She didn't say a word. Lucas said a few comforting things. Pointless things, nothing he could remember five seconds after he had said them. There was nothing really to say. Della nodded, though, half-lost in her own thoughts but appreciating the company. That reassured him a little.

It didn't take long before James announced they were getting close to Maeshowe. Everything was close on these little islands.

Up ahead and to the left, they spotted the flashing of several emergency lights.

"The coppers are already waiting!" Richard said.

"No," James said. "They're beyond Maeshowe, on the road between the Ring of Brodgar and the Standing Stones of Stenness. Something's happened."

After another half kilometer, he cut his lights, as did the column of cars following him, and pulled off to the side of the road.

"From here we walk."

Once they got out of the car, it was easier to see what had happened. From across a broad field, they could see a major accident in the distance, lit by the pulsing lights of several police cars, ambulances, and fire trucks. At least four vehicles had piled up on one another, their hulks obviously twisted and wrecked even from this distance.

"Like the earlier accident we saw," Lucas said.

"It's the ley lines," Della whispered, her voice sounding distant. "They're already lashing out."

They hopped a fence and began walking over a field toward the burial mound's dark bulk. The Orcadians spread out to either side as Lucas and his companions clustered close together.

"Did any of your people die back there?" Lucas asked the fisherman.

"No, thankfully," James said. "Some are in a bad way, though."

"Won't the police see us out here, all exposed like this?"

"With us in the darkness and them standing by all those flashing lights? We need to worry about the ley lines, not the police," Richard said.

And he could already sense it. The ambient energy he had felt on the beach could be felt here, too, and as they approached the burial mound, it only grew.

The sound of screeching tires and crunching metal cut through the night. They turned and saw in the distance two cars entangled in a head-on collision less than a kilometer from the previous accident.

Lucas judged the angle and realized that accident was on the ley line too.

"The normal are beginning to see things," Richard said. "It's leaking out into the mundane world."

"But too much and too fast," James said. "Good old MacHugh could have controlled it, let it out slow to open everyone's eyes without anyone getting hurt. But the old man died and left us with the threat of Armageddon."

"You sure that group from Stromness didn't kill him?" Lucas asked.

"I'm sure. It was just MacHugh's time. He was sickly, the poor gentleman. He should have realized his time was close. I suppose he was too eager to give something back to the world before he died."

The magic around the burial mound was strong enough to set Lucas's teeth on edge. As Richard had predicted, the police, still almost a kilometer away over the field and on a well-lit road, could not see anything of what he and his companions were doing in the dark. One of the Orcadians wiped sweat from his brow then with trembling hands used a power drill to drill through the lock at the entrance to the burial mound. Lucas cast furtive glances at the crash scenes, but the all the noise the emergency crews were making masked the sound of the drill.

In the eerie flashes of the distant emergency

lights, he could see everyone had wide eyes and drawn faces. Lucas realized he must look the same. Everyone could feel the malign influence emanating from Maeshowe. Lucas was amazed the police and ambulance crews couldn't feel it too.

Maybe they can, he mused. *Maybe they just don't know what they're feeling.*

The lock came off with a sharp snap, and the door creaked open. A wave of foul energy wafted out, making them stagger.

"How do we do this?" Della asked.

"We'll walk you through it," James said. "Like we did with the initiation. I'll need all of you, though."

Lucas stepped through the entrance. Every instinct told him to run away screaming and get off this island, but he knew he had to go through with it. As the person in the group least attuned to the magical energy coursing through this burial mound, perhaps he would be in less danger. Well, Sebastian was less attuned than he was, but he didn't see that fellow volunteering.

Immediately upon passing the threshold, Lucas felt all but overcome by nausea. A cold sweat broke out all over his body, and his hands were unsteady as he turned on the flashlight of his mobile phone, only to see the light dim to nothingness barely three paces down the cramped passageway.

"You're brave, Englishman, I'll give you that," James said. He had entered right behind him.

I don't feel brave, Lucas thought. *I'm not even sure I can make it all the way to the main chamber.*

He made it only halfway there before the passageway was suddenly illuminated by the flaming figure of a man.

21

DCI MATTHEWS HAD COME to Orkney to hunt down a group of occultists with the help of the local constabulary and instead found a police department overwhelmed with a spate of inexplicable accidents and panicked calls about strange intruders in people's homes. He had managed to convince his chief of police—thanks to the activities of the local Oxford suspects and the "evidence" he himself had planted on the internet—and had gotten travel funds and a warrant to bring them in for questioning.

He had flown up to Orkney thinking he had this all wrapped up except for a bit of poking around. He felt sure the Kirkwall police would have been investigating the local occult circle, given all the strange things that had been going on.

Instead he found them putting out brush fires.

Traffic accidents had risen exponentially in the past few days, and there had been disappearances of farm animals, and a ship capsized in calm waters close to shore, plus those reports of intruders. Most seemed to be of children or dwarves in dirty clothing and red caps, although one couple strolling along the beach swore they were accosted by a naked man who came out of the sea. If he hadn't known better, DCI Matthews would have thought that someone had just imported a large shipment of magic mushrooms.

Unfortunately for his sanity, he had seen this before, and he couldn't fob it off with an explanation of some class A controlled narcotics. During the London affair, the phone lines had gone crazy with ghost sightings and other paranormal effects. He didn't know how much of that was true and how much of it was trickery on the part of local occultists, but what he had seen at King's Cross station had been real enough.

He gave them Sebastian's tip-off of the break-in he was going to get them to do into MacHugh's house and managed to get himself and an officer on a ferry boat up there to arrest them, but the group had given them the slip.

"They must be hiding on the island somewhere,"

the officer had said. "Or perhaps they paid someone with a boat to take them off. Either way, we'll find them soon enough."

DCI Matthews wasn't so sure. Mr. Camilo and Mr. Lancaster had shown themselves to be resourceful in the past. The Kirkwall police, however, were optimistic. The suspects couldn't get back to Oxford without flying, and the airports had been put on alert. It was, they said, only a matter of time.

Something in his gut told him they didn't have much time.

And now here he was trying to get help from an undermanned police force that had no time for his tales of visiting occultists from the home counties flying up to cause trouble.

But when his fruitless conversation with an obviously exhausted chief of police got interrupted by a report of a four-car pileup "between Maeshowe and the Standing Stones of Stenness," an alarm bell went off in his head.

Anything unusual happening next to two major archaeological sites was enough to arouse his suspicion.

So he had asked to go along. The Kirkwall chief

of police shrugged and said he could use all the help he could get.

DCI Matthews helped take witness statements, which like several other car crashes in recent days, involved tales of someone veering out of their lane and thinking a child was standing in the road.

"The whole island's gone mad," an officer grumbled to him. "Perhaps some of the local teens have decided to play tricks. I don't think it's very funny, though."

It wasn't. Three of the five people involved in the crash had to be taken to hospital, all in critical condition.

Now the emergency services were busy cleaning up the street, and a tow truck had come to pull away the vehicles, all four of which were totaled. DCI Matthews, at loose ends for the moment, stood to one side of the road at the edge of a field, half in the darkness.

A strange prickling at the back of his neck made him turn around. Out in the field, a squat figure in a red cap danced and capered in the light of the emergency vehicles. When it caught the policeman looking, it grinned and waved.

DCI Matthews turned to a paramedic walking by.

"Who's that?" he said, pointing at the figure.

The paramedic looked in the direction he had pointed. "Who's who?"

DCI Matthews was about to sputter a response about how the woman must be blind but stopped.

The little fellow is as clear as day, and yet she can't see it.

His heart went cold.

The woman was still squinting at the field. "Who?" she asked again.

"Nothing," he mumbled. "Trick of the light."

The paramedic moved on.

He looked at the figure again. It motioned for him to come closer.

It?

Yes, he had a feeling this was not a child. Or a man. Or a woman.

But just what the hell was it?

The thing moved off across the field for a few meters then stopped, turned, and motioned for DCI Matthews to follow.

He glanced around. No one was paying any attention to them.

He stepped off the road and with long, quick strides and followed the thing into the dark field.

It did not take long to get out of sight of the emergency response team. The squat figure led him diagonally across a broad field, never uttering a sound.

"Who are you?" DCI Matthews asked. The thing was about ten meters from him. He tried to catch up, but the thing only increased its own pace, its short legs moving remarkably fast.

It did not answer.

"What are you?" he asked.

That earned him a childlike giggle that turned his heart to ice. The thing kept its distance ahead of him.

DCI Matthews put his hand in his pocket where he had his Taser hidden and wished, not for the first time, that he had joined a firearms unit. In his many years as a police officer, there had been more than one incident when he'd really wished he had a firearm. This was the latest.

That feeling was confirmed when he saw where the creature was leading him.

A dark hill stood prominently in the flat field. He'd seen it on the map.

Maeshowe, an ancient burial mound.

When he looked back at the figure he had been following, he found it had vanished.

DCI Matthews stopped in his tracks, looking

around the darkened field. There was little light to see by, but the field was completely open. There was no way the thing could be hiding or have run off in the distance in the two seconds he had taken his eyes off of it.

He studied the burial mound again, visible only as a dark bulk against the slightly lighter sky. The clouds were rolling in low and reflected some of the light of the emergency vehicles, making a pale background to the black hump before him.

Wait, that wasn't the only light. He saw one edge of the burial mound softly glowing, as if from the light of a flashlight or mobile phone. Perhaps more than one. There was a flickering too. Fire?

Whatever it was, it was on the opposite side of the burial mound from where he was. He slowed down, pulling the Taser out of his pocket and moving carefully to avoid making any noise. With his other hand, he pulled a flashlight out of his pocket but did not turn it on yet. He didn't want to signal his presence.

A movement in the shadows to his right made him whip around. He saw two dark forms rise up. He had the impression of two men hunched down in dark coats to hide themselves, but he couldn't see enough to be sure. He flicked on his flashlight...

...and found himself facing down the barrels of two rifles.

"Police officer! Drop your weapons immediately!"

The calm voice that replied had the local Scottish burr. "Terribly sorry, officer. But this is too important to comply. Drop that Taser and I won't hurt you."

"Threatening an officer of the law carries a penalty—"

"That isn't death. If I let you have your way, I'll die. So will you. Drop that Taser."

A madman. One of those occultist madmen.

He dropped the Taser.

"Drop the flashlight too. You're blinding me with that bally thing."

DCI Matthews did as he was told.

The two men approached. One slung his rifle and bent to grab the gear the police officer had dropped. Briefly, DCI Matthews considered kicking him in the face and grabbing his Taser back, but the other man had his rifle trained on him.

Then the completely unexpected happened. DCI Matthews was beginning to expect that.

The small figure in the red cap appeared behind the gunman. Didn't just walk into view but actually *appeared* out of thin air. It was closer than it had been before, and with the light leaking around the far side of the burial mound, the police officer could see it more clearly. It was an ugly thing, with a squat body, broad face, and warty skin. Its clothes looked like those of some medieval peasant, rough home-spun tunic and pants and little pointed boots. DCI Matthews still couldn't tell if it was male or female, or if it was a human or not. Probably not. Humans didn't vanish and then reappear out of nowhere.

With the two gunmen busy concentrating on the police officer, they didn't notice the new arrival. The creature gave him a sly grin and then kicked the gunman covering him in the back of the knees.

The man toppled over. DCI Matthews gave the nearer man the kick in the face he had intended to, scooped up the Taser, and zapped the gunman as he lay sprawled and surprised on the wet grass. Then he spun around and gave the second man a jolt.

DCI Matthews crouched low, scanning the dark for other criminals. He saw no one. The little creature had vanished again. The only sounds were the distant hum of the engines far across the field and some low chanting coming from... somewhere.

Pulling a pair of plastic zip cuffs from his pocket, he flipped over the two stunned occultists and secured their hands behind their backs. Then he picked up one of the rifles, jacked out the bullets, and tossed it as far as he could into the darkness. The second rifle he took.

He held it uncertainly. Picking up a gun in the course of a police investigation was far beyond regulations if you weren't an authorised firearms officer, which he wasn't. DCI Matthews wanted to live, however, and so he had a feeling he might need it.

At least he knew how to shoot. He had been in the Territorial Army for a few years as a younger man. He had never fired a shot in anger, though.

Keeping the gun leveled at the bright edge of the burial mound, he paced slowly toward it, keeping away from the edge of the mound so no one could suddenly come on him from around the corner.

The chanting grew louder, as did the light. He could now see a walkway leading away from the burial mound and off toward another road in the distance.

The light must be coming from inside the Maeshowe mound. They're inside, making magic. Perhaps they're summoning the spirits that have caused all the problems around here.

If he had had that thought a few months before, he would have asked for an appointment with the police department psychologist. Now he had seen a war band of ghostly Celts cut a man apart and had his life saved by a dwarf or a troll or a hobbit or whatever the hell that thing was.

DCI Matthews rounded the edge of the mound and came to where a modern door had been cut into its side. It stood open.

He peered in, and his eyes widened. He faced a long, low passage made of rough stones fitted together without mortar and crowded with more of the miniature people dressed in medieval garb. They turned to him, and all their faces took on anxious looks as they pointed down the passageway in silent alarm.

Then they vanished.

DCI Matthews blinked, his heart skipping a beat.

It almost didn't start beating again when he witnessed what lay down the passageway.

A larger room was at the end, and while he couldn't see it all, he could see enough.

Ms. Marshal and her friends, along with some people he didn't recognize, stood clustered close together, chanting in some weird language. They looked terrified, their drawn faces and bugging eyes illuminated by a flame that was not within his line of sight.

They all stared at the source of that flame, although they continued chanting. No one took any notice of him.

As if in a dream, DCI Matthews hunched over and hurried down the long, low passage. He could feel the heat coming out of what should have been a cold stone chamber and heard the faint crackling of flame, but oddly he did not smell any smoke. He did smell something else, though—a sickly, burnt odor that made his stomach churn.

He had no explanation for that. Hell, he had no explanation for anything anymore.

The police officer came into the main chamber of the burial mound, and his last hold on mundane reality shattered.

Off to one side stood a fiery figure. At first glance, he thought it was a man consumed by fire, but then he realized it was not a man at all but a vaguely humanoid figure made up of lines of fire like the dream of some mad artist. It seemed to be pushing against an invisible barrier, its hands flaring up as it struck against a point in the air. The group of people DCI Matthews had intended on arresting continued to chant in some strange foreign language that sounded vaguely Scandinavian or Germanic.

No, only the strangers chanted. Those he had pursued all the way up here from Oxford were simply standing there, some with their eyes closed, as if meditating. Around them, drawn on the giant flagstones, was a chalk circle decorated with various complex designs that looked a bit like Norse runes. The fiery creature stood just outside it—*a magic circle, like in the old medieval pictures,* DCI Matthews realized—and was banging against the air at a point just above the edge of the circle.

On the other side of chamber lay a badly burnt corpse, its clothes scorched entirely away and its features savaged beyond recognition.

"Everyone stop and put your hands in the air! You are all under arrest!" he shouted, sweeping the room with the rifle.

He realized how ridiculous his words sounded as soon as he said them.

Everyone turned to him. Della and her friends opened their eyes and stared. The others, still chanting, turned and gave him a startled look. Even the fiery figure stopped bashing against the air and seemed to gaze at him.

Sweat poured off his face. The air was stifling in

here, the stench of that poor burn victim over-powering.

"Shoot them!" someone shouted behind him. The accent was strange, the voice high and squeaky. He turned and saw one of the red-capped creatures standing at the entrance. It gave him a pleading look. "Shoot them. Their ritual will destroy the world."

DCI Matthews stepped back. "What the hell are you?"

"Don't step into the circle!" Richard Camilo shouted.

He stopped, glanced at the chalk. His foot was an inch from it. He turned back to the figure.

"We are the spirits of the land," the little creature said. "These evil sorcerers want to destroy the world. They're insane. They want to kill all of humanity."

DCI Matthews glanced at the chanting group huddled within the circle. He saw Sebastian among them—that confused, spoiled toff who had mucked up his relationships and been found drunk and drugged outside a pub in Oxford.

Their eyes locked. The young man was obviously terrified.

Someone like that wouldn't agree to do such a foul thing, but what if he had been forced into it?

His gaze moved from Sebastian to Richard, who

had been arrested many times for sneaking into historic and archaeological monuments to do rituals in the middle of the night.

That had earned him no end of fines, fines he had only paid after giving the arresting officers ridiculous lectures about religious freedom.

Yes, he had been arrested many times, but he had never been convicted of anything but doing weird rituals in ancient sites he took care never to damage. Oh, and for breaking into a pub in order to gain access to some underground tunnels in London, but even then he had stolen nothing, damaged nothing, and had supposedly been searching for a kidnapped victim.

Would someone like him really be engaged in an evil ritual?

Something clicked in DCI Matthews's mind. The troll-like figure still pleading in front of him, the fiery man on the other side of the room that made the interior of the mound sweltering, the magic circle inscribed on the floor... it was all true. He had suspected it before, and now his nose was being rubbed in it. Everything Richard and Lucas had told him had turned out to be true.

They were troublemakers, to be sure, but the

trouble they caused was to ward off far greater trouble.

He rounded on the squat figure in the red cap.

"The ritual is almost done," it pleaded, its eyes going wide on its broad, warty face. "If they finish, they will finish us all."

DCI Matthews pointed the rifle at the troll.

"Hands up. You're under arrest!"

22

DELLA'S CONCENTRATION broke when the police officer burst on the scene. She felt the strength of the ritual waver. James, the Orcadians, Cassandra, Lucas, and Richard had kept their focus, but they had lost Della's participation and that weakened the force of the magic. She could feel the foul forces swirling around the interior of Maeshowe drawn inward, pressing at the edge of the magical circle.

She struggled to maintain her focus. The Orcadians had warned her that for the ritual to work, for them to switch off the spell MacHugh had set into motion, they'd need every bit of their strength.

She'd started to lose her focus when one of the Orcadian sentries rushed in saying they'd been attacked, and the fire spirit James had banished when they first entered had immediately reappeared and killed the sentry. She'd clenched her eyes and stopped up her ears so as not to witness his horrible death and reassured herself the thing couldn't make it across the magical circle, that she and her friends were safe as long as they continued with the ritual.

And then that police officer had run in and pointed a gun at them.

She didn't know much about magic, but she suspected magical circles weren't bulletproof.

Then the troll appeared and tried to trick him. The man had hesitated and then tried to arrest a *genius loci* in the semblance of a folkloric creature.

It would have been laughable if it hadn't put the entire world into grave peril.

When the officer turned his rifle on the troll, several things happened all at the same time.

The troll laughed in the man's face and leapt forward. The gun went off, and at that range, the bullet must have hit, but the troll seemed unaffected as it pushed the police officer back.

Straight across the protective circle.

The man's shoe scraped the chalk barrier, erasing it.

A magical creature couldn't come close, but an ordinary man could destroy the powerful sigils as easily as if they were a child's drawing on a playground.

The troll laughed and capered with glee, and suddenly the entrance passageway swarmed with them. The fire spirit stepped forward, hands flaring.

James Firth and Richard shouted out a power word at the same time. Force rippled out from the circle like a shock wave. The fire spirit flew back, fading, its lines of fire unraveling, but it did not disappear. The crowd of trolls staggered and stopped in their tracks.

"Close the circle!" Sebastian wailed.

"It doesn't work that way," Lucas said. "Once broken, the whole ritual has to be begun again."

He said something more, but Della couldn't hear him with that cop blasting away at the fire spirit.

The bullets, of course, did nothing. The fire spirit began to reform.

James and Richard didn't have the strength to banish it again. Not if they wanted to maintain the push of the ritual to stop MacHugh's spell.

And if they stopped doing that, the whole effort would collapse, and that poor man killed by the fire spirit would have died for nothing.

Everyone would die for nothing.

She had to do something, but what? She was

trying to focus her energy on the ritual the Orca-dians had started, a ritual she didn't understand but could feel in her bones. As they had started, she could feel the ley lines begin to power down, she could feel the toxicity of the earth's power grid begin to lessen. The ritual was working. She couldn't stop now. But how could she defend herself if those creatures came rushing at them again?

And they would. The trolls were already regrouping. The fire spirit was glowing brighter, its flaming lines coalescing into a more solid form.

They needed more power if they were going to take care of both threats at the same time.

She turned to Sebastian, who was standing there shaking. He hadn't participated in the ritual at all. The only reason he was inside the circle was to keep him safe.

His power only comes when he's in mortal danger. That's what Richard said.

"Get ready," she told him as, with a strength born of fear, she grabbed him by the shoulders and shoved him at the fire spirit.

Sebastian let out a squawk and stumbled right for the thing. For a moment, Della hissed in terror, thinking she had just killed her ex-boyfriend.

And then Sebastian's energy lit up like an arc lamp.

It was almost a visible thing, a surge in power so great that it made everyone in the now-useless circle stumble one or two steps away.

Sebastian cried out and pushed at the fire spirit, actually shoved it like it was a normal human being. The spirit flew back against the wall and vanished with a whoosh and a waft of brimstone, leaving a burnt silhouette as the only evidence of its passing.

"Go away!" he screamed. The trolls scattered, running in a disorganized mass for the passageway.

The ley lines convulsed, the ground rocking in a very physical tremor. Della looked up at the ancient masonry as dirt trickled through the gaps in the stone. This monument had stood for thousands of years, but it had probably never been subjected to forces such as those passing through it now.

"Focus!" one of the Orcadians shouted.

The ley line grew in strength, the taint in its power making Della wretch, her knees going weak. Sebastian fell, his face wracked with pain and exhaustion. One of the Orcadians collapsed.

The Orcadians resumed their chanting in Old Norse. The strength of their ritual began to stabilize, pressing down the rising taint of the ley lines.

The nexus redoubled its strength. The network of ley lines acted like a living thing, as if they had sensed Sebastian had fought off the creatures in the tomb and now the lines themselves were summoning the strength to get rid of these interfering humans.

Della focused. Although she had been initiated into the Orcadian Rite, she didn't know any of the rituals. It was like being handed a degree in electrical engineering and told to fix a power station. She could only try and lend her own force of will to those more knowledgeable around her.

It felt like it was working. The taint of the nexus began to subside. She could feel the power of the ritual push down on it like a wrestler who had finally gotten on top and pinned his opponent down.

But it was slow, grinding work. The pressure of the nexus took all their energy, all their willpower, all their concentration.

And then that concentration snapped as a troll appeared in the middle of the broken circle and leapt onto James's back, sinking its yellow, snaggled teeth into his neck.

James cried out. He had been the leader of the ritual, the most powerful person chanting, and his focus shattered.

Just like everyone else's. They sprang back from

the creature or glanced around, fearful of another popping into sight. None came. The ley lines were using most of their strength to shake off this trouble-some race on their planet and only spared enough to materialize one creature to disrupt the ritual.

It was enough. Everyone was panicking now or trying individual efforts that did not add up to nearly enough power. Only Lucas had the presence of mind to smack at the troll, using his Talent as much as his fist to knock the hideous thing off James's back...

...only to have it leap on him.

The ley line's power swelled. Nausea almost overcame Della. A couple of the Orcadians fell to their knees. If the nexus wasn't stopped right now, Della sensed it would all be over. But the troll had thrown Lucas to the ground and was choking him. He'd die in another couple of seconds.

She could save Lucas or try and stabilize the ritual. She didn't have the time or the energy to do both.

She tried to do both anyway.

Della took a deep breath, closed her eyes to the chaos around her, ignored her shaking legs and churning stomach, and summoned the very last of her willpower.

She imagined it all balled up in her head. With a

sudden effort, she brought it smacking down on the floor like an upside-down nuclear explosion, its force spreading out with unstoppable fury. Even with her eyes closed, she saw the troll get knocked back out of this plane of existence. The rising power of the nexus got clamped down, not gone but temporarily stunned.

And then more power joined her own. She felt Richard and Cassandra add their power to hers, and then some of the Orcadians. Lucas joined in, and Sebastian recovered enough to lend an inexperienced hand. The chanting resumed, but by then, it was barely needed.

Della felt something strange. As the taint in the ley lines withered, she felt another surge of power trying to push it down. It came from the other side of the island. How she could know this, she wasn't sure. Another group had added its strength to theirs.

The Stromness group, it must be, Della thought. *They finally saw who was winning and picked the right side.*

Better late than never.

The ley lines eased down in power. The taint disappeared. The network of earth energy ringing the globe became neutral again.

But Della didn't feel that. She had passed out.

She came to with Lucas holding her and shouting into her face.

"Are you all right? Della, say something!" He said it like he had said it several times already.

"Stop screaming in my face."

"You did it!"

Now that she was conscious again, she could feel that everything was back to normal. "We did it."

Richard's face appeared. "More you than us. I'm surprised you didn't burn yourself out."

"I feel... strange," Della said.

"You do." Richard frowned. "The magical energy radiating from you feels different somehow."

"Could someone please tell me what the hell just happened?"

They turned. The police officer stood not far off, still gripping his useless rifle.

Richard grinned. "Good to see you again, DCI Matthews. Isn't it awful when a repeat offender's supposedly unbelievable alibis turn out to be true?"

DCI Matthews was slightly paler than your average ghost.

"It's all real," he said in a soft voice. "Magic and trolls and demons are all real."

"Yes, they are," Lucas said. "I think we're going to need to sit down and have a long chat."

The police officer looked around at the scorched body and the black silhouette in the wall.

"I'm going to have a devil of a time explaining this to my chief," DCI Matthews complained. "You two are trouble to everyone around you."

"I can vouch for that," Della said as Lucas helped her to her feet.

"Hey!" Richard cried. "You had fun saving the world. Don't deny it."

Della glanced at the terrible sight of the burnt Orcadian man. "It's not fun at all."

James walked over to the body and looked down at it. "Poor Harold Ruskin. He was a good man and a good practitioner." He turned and looked Della in the eye. "He died doing what he loved, doing what he was good at, and he died saving his friends and family. He wouldn't have wanted it any other way. Don't mourn him, just honor his memory. He's fully in the spirit world now. Death is terrible, yes, but it is not the end."

Quite true, a voice said in her head. Della jerked with surprise as she recognized it as Montague's. *I'm off to where I should be now. Thank you for releasing me.*

"I didn't do anything," she said out loud, drawing curious looks from everyone.

Ah, but you did. I had tied myself to those books. I worried that someone might steal them, so I put my own personal energy into the ward. I forgot to unlink that when we went into danger in London, and when I was pushed to the other side, the link remained. I was stuck between worlds, and that muddled my mind so much I didn't know what had gone wrong. Then the ley lines tried to reach through to me and force me to do their will. Now that the books are safe and the ley lines calm, I am free.

"Goodbye," Della said, a lump forming in her throat.

Take care of your friends. They need you.

23

LUCAS COULDN'T BELIEVE what he had witnessed. It had been far beyond anything he had ever experienced, even worse than that terrifying night in his childhood.

Even three days later, sitting in Montague's house in London, he still felt shaken and drained.

The double silhouette of the fire spirit on the living room wall sure didn't help his mood. Why did Richard insist on sitting here?

At least he was getting some of Montague's calming herbal tea. He hoped Richard would brew up about three more kettles of it.

"No sign of our friend," Richard said, nodding to the mark of the creature on the wall. "I think the Stromness occult circle has laid off."

"They should have been helping us instead of looking out for themselves."

"You know how people are, especially in the occult community. I got a call from James, our dour old fisherman friend. Some of his crew went over to Stromness and gave them a good talking to."

"Better them than me. I'd have wanted to beat them black-and-blue."

"I think that's what Scottish fishermen mean when they say 'a good talking to.'"

"Good. Do you think Sebastian called the police on us?" Lucas asked, changing the subject to something that had been foremost in his mind for the past three days. "If he did, I'd like to beat him to within an inch of his life and send him up to James for a second round."

Richard shook his head. "I don't think it matters anymore."

"How can you say that? Who could it have been except Sebastian? They knew we were headed to Stronsay before we even boarded the ferry. Sebastian is dangerous, I'm telling you."

"More to himself than anyone else," Richard said softly. "I've never seen a Talent like his. More powerful than anyone I've ever seen, even Della, but completely unpredictable. I'm going to have to keep a close eye on him so he doesn't get pulled into the wrong circle."

Lucas wasn't listening. "All those times he went to his room or the pub supposedly to see that Danish git? I bet he was calling the Oxford police. DCI Matthews must have been flying up just as we headed to Stronsay for him to have gotten to Maeshowe in time to interfere. That Oxford copper nearly ruined the whole ritual."

Richard raised a calming hand. "But he didn't. In fact, he helped, both in the fight and in covering up everything later."

Lucas grinned. "Did you see James's face when we found two of his pals Tased and handcuffed outside the mound?"

Richard laughed. "Priceless!"

"You should have let me question Sebastian," Lucas said, his hands balling into fists.

"We had a nearly catatonic American, a panicky police officer, and a dead body to deal with."

"I could have questioned him afterward."

"When? The next morning? The flight? We had to deal with a slightly less catatonic American, a nosy Dane who wanted to know what had happened to the national monument in his care, and a police officer who wanted a crash course in occultism from people he kept threatening to arrest. But it all worked out in the end. We made it through and stopped MacHugh's spell. Only a few people died instead of a few billion."

Lucas grew serious. "I didn't do enough. I wasn't ready for magic on that level."

"Honey, I've been doing this since you were in grade school and I wasn't ready either."

"No, I really wasn't helping enough. Aunt Mary is right. I need to take on my responsibility. I need to study more so I can be ready next time, because there will be a next time." He looked his friend in the eye. "I need to be initiated."

Richard chuckled and put a hand on his shoulder. "Well, it's about time. Don't worry, my friend, I'll take care of that."

HIDING in her room in Oxford surrounded by books had lost its appeal. Attending lectures given by learned professors who only saw half of reality no longer interested her.

Della had changed.

At first she thought it had only been a reaction to the danger and terror of what had occurred in

Orkney, but now she realized it ran far deeper than that. She saw things differently now, not only with her intellect, but literally with her eyes. Passing by St. Edmund's, one of Oxford's medieval colleges, she had spotted the pale image of a woman in medieval garb at one of the windows. The old Della would have dismissed that as imagination or some undergraduate prank. The new Della looked up ghost hauntings at Oxford colleges and found a legend of a gray lady who appeared sometimes at that very same window.

It was on her way home, and she had passed that window hundreds of times. She had never seen anything before.

The next night she saw the same figure, and she knew that she would see the gray lady every time she passed that window after dark.

And then she had a dream of Bjorn calling her from the Reel while local folk music played in the background.

The next evening, Bjorn called her. She could hear that very same tune in the background and did not need to ask him where he was calling from.

The poor guy thought she was still in Orkney and wanted to ask her out on a date. She gave some lame excuse about a sick uncle back in Oxford, even though he knew all her relatives were in the States, and hung up.

Poor Bjorn. He was too nice of a guy to get wrapped up in all this.

Because there was no getting out of it for her now.

Overextending herself in the ritual had changed something. She was connected to the hidden world permanently now, a bit like that little girl in the folk-tale with the crow's head. Della's ties to the magical world weren't as obvious, but they were no less strong.

Della decided to skip her lectures the following day and go see Aunt Mary up at the farm. She had a lot of studying to do.

DCI MATTHEWS HAD NEVER BEEN MUCH of a drinker, but he really, really wanted to get soused on the job today.

He had suffered a tongue-lashing from his chief of police over wasting police funds on a "wild-goose chase to the far north when you should have been taking care of your own patch right here in Oxford." That had been somewhat ameliorated by a call from the Kirkwall chief of police explaining how he had chased off some intruders at Maeshowe who looked ready to destroy a priceless archaeological site.

Even so, it didn't look like DCI Matthews would be getting a pay rise this year.

It was hard to care about such things with the memory of the Maeshowe fight seared into his mind's eye.

The last shred of doubt had been torn from his psyche. It was all real.

And there was only one thing to do—stamp out the trouble wherever it occurred. There was no way he could convince his colleagues, so he would have to do it himself. That was what he had been thinking when this whole sorry affair began, and he felt twice as committed now.

At least now he knew what he was up against.

In the course of his investigations into the occult circles of London and the surrounding area, he had not come up with evidence to arrest Mr. Lancaster and Mr. Camilo like he had wanted to. Instead, he had come up with a dozen trails of evidence linking strange groups and practices to any number of crimes. None of these trails had any solid proof. None of them had enough to warrant getting funding and manpower from his chief. But now that

DCI Matthews was looking at his job with a new set of eyes, he knew in his gut that many of the patterns he was seeing were real. Those occultists he had wanted to arrest and ended up helping only saw their small part of the picture. He was seeing the whole thing. The picture was blurry. It was vague, and he didn't really understand what he was looking at. But there was no doubting that occultists in England were involved in any number of crimes.

Mr. Lancaster and Mr. Camilo—and yes, Ms. Marshal—would help him see the picture more clearly.

He picked up the telephone to call them, but not to haul them down to the station for questioning. No, this time, they were coming as allies.

They had a lot of work to do together.

ABOUT THE AUTHOR

S.A. Beck lives in sunny California. When she's not surfing, knitting, or daydreaming in a hammock, she's writing novels.

www.sabeckbooks.com